SERGIO CHEJFEC is the author of eighteen
books of fiction, poetry and essays. Born in
Argentina, he lived in Venezuela from 1990
to 2005 and since then has resided in New
York City, where he is Distinguished Writer
in Residence at New York University. He
has received fellowships from the Civitella
Ranieri Foundation and from the John
Simon Guggenheim Foundation. Chejfec's
text-based installation *Dissemination of
a Novel* was featured at the 2016 Kochi-
Muziris Biennale in India. His novels *My Two
Worlds*, *The Dark* and *The Planets* have been
published in English translation.

MARGARET CARSON has translated
Sergio Chejfec's *My Two Worlds*. She teaches
at the City University of New York.

Also from
ALMOST ISLAND BOOKS

Trying to Say Goodbye
by Adil Jussawalla

Five Movements in Praise
by Sharmistha Mohanty

Magadh
by Shrikant Verma
translated from the Hindi by Rahul Soni

Blind Screens
by Ranjani Murali

BARONI
A JOURNEY

SERGIO
CHEJFEC

BARONI, A JOURNEY
by Sergio Chejfec
English translation by Margaret Carson

ISBN 978-81-921295-4-9
First Edition, First Printing 2017

Published by Almost Island Books
Flat 214, Binayak Residency
6/5D, Anil Moitra Road
Kolkata 700019, India
www.almostisland.com
almostisland.edit@gmail.com

Original text © Sergio Chejfec
English translation © Margaret Carson
Publisher of Spanish edition: Alfaguara Argentina (2007)

Book and cover design by Siddhartha Chatterjee
sc@seechange.in

Printing coordination by Milan Bhattacharjee
Printed by Sonu Printers
B-180, Okhla Industrial Area, Phase-1
New Delhi 110020, India

Typeset in Arno Pro and Bell Gothic by TheSeeChange.com

BARONI
A JOURNEY

SERGIO
CHEJFEC

Translated from the Spanish by
MARGARET CARSON

ALMOST ISLAND BOOKS
2017

I have before me the wooden body of the saint; the wood
has cracked down the middle of this doctor who looks
straight out ahead without seeing anything in particular.

During his physical life, the great man divided his
time into three known parts (or his known time into
three parts): the poor and sick, science, and God. Later,
after he died and his fame slowly grew as a protector,
an effective guardian of health, and even a healer, he
abandoned science and protected the not so needy as
well with his spiritual gift. The wooden figure is some
eighty centimeters tall and carries in its arms a child
that clings to the doctor's left front side, as if seeking
to flatten itself against his body. The child turns out
to be the Child, no further introductions necessary.
The black frock coat the doctor wore throughout his
physical life is also with him here; the coat sheathes
his body, as is almost always the case with this doctor,
invariably calling to mind the urbane, cosmopolitan
elegance he practiced with habitual discipline, to which
end he had his suits tailored from patterns out of Paris.
As I said, the wood has cracked. It seems, however,
a benevolent wound, or at any rate an obliging one,
because it gets muddled with the line of buttons on his
coat. As the crack ascends, it runs alongside his black
tie and proceeds less unnoticeably into his neck, where
it dies out in a sudden cleft. There is another crack,
disconcerting because it looks violent, that splits the
right ear in two and rises toward the parietal bone until

vanishing, or erasing itself, under the hat, also black, that covers his head. That hat is another of the characteristic elements; and in practice there is no scenario in which the great man fails to wear one. Lower down, the crack in the middle takes leave of the coat and partitions the groin badly. In this area the body has been forgotten, no bulk is suggested, and that makes the fissure look deep, more private, perhaps alluding to a latent nakedness, or rather, to an innocent nakedness.

It is curious to note the slight twist in his left shoulder, a movement that bespeaks the act of holding up the child. When I've happened to observe how other people react to the figure, I've found in their eyes, and in certain of their almost imperceptible gestures, first surprise, and then admiration at this fact. And I also found, among those who had perceived nothing of the kind, an active interest, a sort of curiosity they found hard either to satisfy or to ascribe to something in particular, and which was no doubt due to the nature of this artistic, or dramatic, inspiration assigned to the body of the doctor. A body liberated from the priestly mien that generally accompanies him in the millions of figures of every type in which he looks stiff, like a small tutelary deity. I have another variant of the saint's body; I could describe its unusually active pose – and I say unusual because it's a bit dynamic: one leg is poised to walk, and the back leans forward, as if climbing a hill – but I won't do so now, perhaps later on.

The Child clings to the body of the saint, for a moment he seems entirely devoted to listening to the heart of his protector. His left arm embraces the doctor, and the right one, imprisoned between the two bodies as it is, has no choice but to aim upward; then the arm flexes and the Child puts his hand on his head, as if he were resting, adopting a forced posture that expresses calm

and discomfort at once. He looks up at the face of the
saint, and on his red-painted lips one discerns a smile of
satisfaction, or rather of relief, as if beside the doctor he
had found the refuge denied him until that moment by
the rest of the land and its people. This might sound like
an exaggeration, there's no way to prove the Child indeed
lacked shelter in any other place, but still it is a truth
that leaps from the figure. In the meantime, the saint's
imperturbable gaze says, or so I believe, 'Don't worry,
you're here now,' or something like that.

Despite his monumental bearing and his striking attire,
the doctor tends toward absence wherever he is placed.
It's a dispassionate mien, not very forthcoming, and one
doesn't know whether to attribute it to disorientation or
rigidity. For this same reason he could be a literary hero,
one of those who are always submissive, contemplative,
indifferent, absorbed by unending meditations. The child
is dressed in a tunic that comes down to his ankles; I
have no better way to describe it than to call it biblical
or pastoral; it is sky blue and at its waist one can hardly
detect the golden ribbon that girds it. The child's bare
feet peek out, with their tiny toes and their frankly
microscopic toenails painted red, barely a thin line.
These feet, too, cleave to the doctor's body, they even
seem to clutch it, and might be another way of showing
the child's forlornness, the need for comfort that inhabits
every inch of his skin. The saint, so citified, and the child,
so rural. There's a detail on the child's skirt, a tropical
bird wrought at the height of his shinbone. It's a small
blue and red macaw, with some yellow as well.

Rafaela Baroni includes one of these birds on every piece
she makes. She calls them 'little parrots'; for her it's a
matter of adding a parrot, which turns out to be always
more or less the same animal in a renewed presentation.
When we spoke by phone once, she told me she'd had

no room for the parrot on this now damaged saintly doctor and so thought she'd have to content herself with painting one on. It would not be long before I finally saw the figure; moreover, as I'll probably explain later, it was a piece of information she'd already given me; but I'm recalling the comment now because of the familiarity with which she spoke of these immovable characters. Baroni, however, succeeded in making a not merely superficial parrot, because she ended up carving it in relief on the child. Life is related to volume; superficiality is a subterfuge, a mere representation, or better yet, a cover up. The parrot becomes bodily real if it appears in three dimensions; if not, it serves as a simple euphemism.

The other piece by Baroni that is in my power, that is also 'mine' (I'll probably explain later what I mean by the quotation marks), shows a woman leaning against the trunk of a putative tree that has only two short, thick limbs, actually, a roughhewn piece of wood in the form of an irregular cross. The work, as I remember, is called the woman on the cross, or the crucified woman – Baroni, for her part, is not indifferent to the two names: she prefers the second; I, for a fairly obvious reason, prefer the first. This piece has its parrot: it looks out from one of the stubby limbs of the tree. The woman does just the same, she looks ahead of her. Like the saintly doctor, she gives the impression of being in a dispassionate ecstasy, the sort of absent mien that, in effect, seems like a dramatic, actorly gesture, the pose the character has taken in order to display herself. The fact is, at a certain moment Baroni's figures tend to come to life. This is not reflected in any unlikely movement, of course, but instead above all in their equilibrium and restraint: they adopt a quiet, ambivalent life, similar in certain respects to that of rocks or objects, but also to that of those beings who inhabit borderlands, lethargic, unmoving and paradoxically omniscient. The Brazilian Cabral spoke of stones, of their unemphatic presence. Baroni's pieces possess something of that irresolute expression, settled into time and condemned not to change, I mean, exposed to their own immobility.

The woman on the cross is one of the few figures made by Baroni that has an anonymous source, or at any rate an undefined one, and lacks a proper name. The others, when they are women, are Virgins, and when they are men they are saints (either recognized by the Church or popular ones, like the doctor). I'm acquainted with other pieces as well, but these don't exactly represent people, or at least entire bodies; one of them is a shoe; the other, a cranium or bare head. And as always, the everlasting parrots, which I sometimes think are affixed to the bodies so as to defend their own changeless world, safe and sound and keeping a sharp eye on the evolution of saints and people. Baroni's wooden shoe stands out as a curious thing, maybe aberrant as well, because it isn't merely a shoe that she carved with lesser or greater effort, but instead it accompanies, or rather contains, a foot (also of wood). A shoe in name only, because actually it's a woman's sandal, high-heeled, with two or three leather or cloth straps. I imagine Baroni must have foreseen the challenge, or for her, the unclear sense, that lurked in the act of carving the sandal empty, and must have thus decided that it would contain a foot with its toes and toenails, chiseled broadly, which at the top exhibits a smoothness that at first looks cosmetic, something closer to wax. To me that shoe has often seemed the excuse for the foot, the subterfuge or pretext for making it, of course, but also so as not to show it undefended.

As far as I know, the cranium and the foot conceal no individual, there's no one behind those pieces of wood turned into an isolated physical presence and incomplete bodily form. That's why these works prove a bit unusual, because Baroni is not an artist in the habit of offering general arguments, I mean abstract or conceptual propositions: at most, she indicates, describes, at the very most enunciates, her main goal being the virtuous glorification issuing from the world of religion, beyond that never making any objection to or critique of anything that could be considered negative. The world of Baroni is large but circumscribed, conscious of its limits and always populated by good and clear intentions. The shoe and the head also draw attention because of another unexpected circumstance, the austerity of the composition: coloration is nearly absent, nor do the typical features of Baroni's costumes appear, there are no vivid colors, no added artifice or ornamental minutia, etc. I imagine that by her own creative logic – by that which took the lead as she made these two pieces, at least – whatever is not for some reason strongly determined must be exaggeratedly indeterminate, with no gradations possible. At the same time, for Baroni, I also think, every human figure calls for a definition, the bestowing of a name, first of all, and secondly, the playing of a role: something that grants existence to that piece of wood. That being the case, the only way to avoid this injunction of totality was the partial representation of the body, abstraction as a loan of the parts. In this way one can see how artists naturally gravitate toward indeterminacy, it's a force that draws them beyond their expressive consciousness, even in the cases when their nature, as in Baroni's case, dictates the opposite.

That's why the woman on the cross seemed fairly singular, and that thought occurred as soon as I saw her. And also owing to a further detail, which makes her kindred with the sizable entourage of Virgins Baroni has made, all severe and in appearance far removed from the blessedness or grace of virginity, their mouths in a rictus that is neither of compassion nor indulgence, but instead of indifference or even outright disinterest, as if they were constantly distracted, focused on their solitary condition, and therefore alien to any possibility of human or spiritual interchange. What that other detail consists of is the fact that each female figure carved by Baroni is a representation of herself. They are self-portraits with different designations (which moreover, as I may describe later, are translated in turn into only a handful of names, I mean the habitual characters of Baroni's iconography); not to mention that the male figures as well almost always seem to have her face, as is the case of the saintly doctor that stands before me. The contoured hair and sparse mustache manage to adhere to the conventions of the figure, and if you forget the devotional image as accepted by the faithful and imagine the saintly doctor hatless and with long hair, you discover Baroni, ready to be a Virgin and rapt with anticipation. At times I've placed the woman on the cross and the saintly doctor side by side, and I've always been astonished by the similarity of their faces, at first with surprise and then, to some degree, with uneasiness.

That hasn't happened only to me, but is the opinion of many other people on seeing both pieces side by side. For example, one morning when the sun was hiding every now and then behind medium-sized clouds in constant motion, which brought about moments of sunlight and of fainter brightness, it seemed to me that the figures had swapped their clothing and accessories, and had each assumed the other's pose and without further ado assumed the role of its partner. So similar did the faces become that the changes in light made them even more identical; or rather, the variations showed that the difference was in the end insignificant, that the faces were right there, available, and that either could have been the face of the other. Children, of course, are the exception. The child in the saintly doctor's arms bears no resemblance to Baroni, nor does any other representation of a child that I recall at the moment, generally also in the arms or on the laps of Virgins or angels. During his physical lifetime, the doctor would pinch the cheeks of children so hard that they feared him or would hide immediately when he entered their homes. That was one of the darker points of his incorruptible goodness, a goodness that was praised by all. The children couldn't understand why he pinched them so hard. But since faces generally lose their chubby cheeks after toddlerhood, these cruelties of the saintly doctor were an experience that left no physical trace among the children themselves, and so in most cases ended up watered down into an object of individual memory.

There could be a materialist explanation for that indistinguishability, or rather permanent likeness of the faces: Baroni refined her manual technique so as to resolve, almost always in the same way, the human countenance. The first time she did it, probably owing to a bout of discouragement that placed her at the limits of her powers, she must have chosen to depict herself in the role of a pious person, suffering and stoic, as a type of release and expiation. Then the custom became ingrained, or the conviction that her own image was the most natural and obvious one, because it was definitely the face that took shape with almost no deliberate intervention; it was skill alone at work, much like automatic speech. We can see that on this point the materialist explanation approaches the other, let's say, spiritual hypothesis, according to which moral inspiration reaches its highest degree of certainty at the moment of artistic execution, when it asserts itself as technical intuition. In this case it is most likely an unconscious replication: in the effort to represent an individual's most characteristic trait, which is to say the face, Baroni obeys an order over which she has no control, under whose guidance she keeps refining the features (foreseeable but each time original) of the new figure. One question would be the following: when is a character more true to life or best achieved – when it is given the materialist explanation, or the spiritual one? Many will regard this question, which springs from the belief that the two explanations prompt different outcomes, as impertinent.

It is very likely Baroni would show no interest in this kind of commentary; she might incline toward a third option, more or less free-floating, which would play different roles according to the circumstance and in which the artist, in the sense of creator, would emerge sometimes as a character and sometimes as a real person (understanding her to be someone capable of extracting herself from the constructed world, whether real or fictional). In this way, Baroni's creations derive from the changeable character she has created, one that coincides intermittently with her own persona. Something perhaps somewhat similar to those stones takes place; Baroni at times chooses an unemphatic presence, hidden behind the figures she has worked on for weeks, and at other times acts as an administrator of identities, distributing attributes and virtues among the creatures she's made. It's an ambiguity latent in the inanimate, much as the poet Cabral noted; when he referred to unemphatic stone, he underscored that what is inert in nature intrigues the most, it conceals a code whose value is the world's permanence. (In another poem he speaks of the hen's egg, and says among other things that, at first sight, it exhibits the autistic inadequacy of stones, with no inside and outside, or in any case with no relevant inside and outside; but, he adds, whoever hefts an egg is amazed by its complex condition as finished form and living organism.)

I met Baroni when she was recovering from a respiratory ailment that had kept her in the hospital for two weeks and left her barely able to speak. When I introduced myself, she began without preamble the story of her convalescence. She told me among other things that I'd found her at home by chance, for the doctors had predicted she'd be staying in the hospital for a third week; but the day before, without much of an explanation, they had authorized her discharge. So Rogelio packed up her hospital garb in the same sports bag they had arrived with, and shortly past noon they left the hospital, walking slowly under the sun, straight to the taxi stand. Baroni was hoarse, the irritation of her larynx had caused her to lose her voice, a state to which she had by now become sadly accustomed. To hear her one had to bend down and bring one's ear a few centimeters from her lips, which turned the conversation into an arduous chain of repetitive motions; not to mention the times Baroni had to repeat her words, which contributed to her fatigue, and the times one had to draw closer to her again, as if her mouth were a broken-down oracle that by a defect or from overuse was unable to do its job. It proved almost impossible for me to understand anything coherent, because I missed a great deal of what she said; and that led me to respond with generalities or to agree in a vague fashion, all of which meant that the most arduous part of the conversation had to be carried on by the person least able to do so.

Months earlier I'd witnessed a similar episode, when the host's difficulty in hearing imposed several specific rules of mobility. We had gathered one afternoon at the home of the poet Juan Sánchez Peláez; there were five of us. By then his illness was well advanced, which kept him from going outdoors. As I say, he couldn't hear well, much less well in one ear than the other; and as happens in those cases, certain voices were clearer to him and he distinguished them better. It was said that Sánchez exaggerated his deafness at times to avoid conversations on subjects that bored him, or recovered his hearing once a few drinks roused him from the lethargy to which his confinement had accustomed him. (Based on my experience that afternoon, I take no position on the matter.) On that occasion, after drinking a bit and taking part in the conversation distractedly, Sánchez began to direct a strange choreography: whenever somebody wanted to speak, that person had to sit to his left; and because there were no extra chairs we had to change places continually to keep the conversation going. It was strange to see an almost diminutive being, like a child no older than ten, be the cause of an operation resembling a children's game, a bit like musical chairs, though in a conversational version. Noises and hearing were always decisive elements for Sánchez, at times problematic. Some years earlier, he'd decided to move from a house he'd lived in for quite a while because of the serenade of small frogs in Caracas at night, at times earsplitting.

In any case, what had seemed to me perhaps necessary at Sánchez's house (collective motion as a means of compensating for his difficulty), though a little eccentric, too, a sort of theatrical whimsy on the part of the poet, as if his visitors were creatures seeking to be coordinated and organized in space, a whimsy that several entered into with enthusiasm, others with resignation, had now at Baroni's house resolved itself far more simply, perhaps owing to its spaciousness and to nature's proximity. The parcel of land on which Baroni built her house manages to be a small-scale world. Her singular imagination moves her to divide up the land into sections and to mark off areas for an array of purposes. I'll probably refer to these divisions, a veritable geography, later on. For now I'll say that the so-called open air, the presence of the intense heat hovering over the greenery of trees and bushes, and of course the noisy, but now-indistinguishable song of the cicadas, all that background buzzing affected Baroni's weakened voice still more.

It was not long before Sánchez Peláez's hour arrived, so to speak, and he died. When I reached the funeral home, in the early hours of the morning, I was struck not so much by the solitude of the place as by the very expressive presence of the nocturnal song he'd fled from whenever possible, as if this animalistic farewell were being enacted on an ironic stage. I saw him in his coffin. As I later found out, the poet had been truly decked out to shine, as they say, in his final resting place, with his favorite safari jacket on. He always had his safari jacket on. You'll rarely find a photo of Sánchez in which he's not wearing one, and that's how it had been ever since his youth, the years he lived in Chile, about which he otherwise had rather bitter memories, those years having been decisive. But now at his wake he wore his best safari jacket, his most classic and impeccable, of a darkish, natural color, and because of the whole mortuary-makeup business it almost matched the coloring of what you could see of his face and hands, which were crossed at his waist. Sanchez's skin looked like wax; and while I didn't bring myself to prove it, though I was tempted, you could divine the almost artificial smoothness of that face, as if funereal conditioning were the first, most urgent thing removing us from nature. The jacket's buttons were of shiny metal and, another tribute to his bohemian elegance, a silk cravat was knotted around his neck, half-hidden under the jacket. A few friends of the deceased were drinking whisky out of disposable cups, from a bottle someone carried hidden in a small shoulder bag, in a kind of prolonged clandestine toast whose privacy, I imagine, was more a tribute to the poet than obedience to any so-called propriety in which none of those present, living or dead, believed.

Recently, my friend Victoria told me about the day Sánchez bought that jacket. She went with him, along with Malena, his wife, to a shopping mall. Through the building's open roof a few clouds could be seen, and higher up, the sky, almost blinding at that midday hour. The color of the sky, and the beauty of being able to observe it through something like an aperture, as if from an observatory, took up a good deal of the conversation while they had a coffee. Afterward they stopped in front of a store and Sánchez needed hardly any time at all to pick out the jacket. The sleeves were long on him, so they took his arm measurements. Some days later he went back for it, this time only with Malena. On their first visit to the mall, neither Victoria nor Malena had any idea of the ultimate fate of the garment, they thought it was just one more of Sánchez's safari jackets. But because of later events, Victoria assumes that her friend already knew the future, in some respect imminent, and was making his decisions. For her part, Malena needed only a few days to realize what was about to happen, and those days coincided with the gap between the first and the second visit to the mall. So the two of them went to pick up the jacket, knowing it would have slight but everlasting use.

In repose, Sánchez's body looked even smaller than it had been during his final days; his shoes were impeccable too. Looking him over for a few moments, with no one else in the room to distract from the communication, the whole of him seemed to me in the first place like a fabricated being, some species of body created in the image of the real Sánchez, hidden nonetheless within that human covering. This new format had forced him to shrink, paying something like a physical tariff, in body mass, for having deigned to become a copy and a representation. I paused for a while on the funeral home's veranda, where the friends I mentioned were gathered, and we made two toasts to the memory of Sánchez, interlarding the conversation in an obvious way with lines of his that were well-known, and even unknown. I had two glasses of the goodbye liquor. From this place one could see the giant trees of the avenue, where almost exclusively, and from time to time, large and dilapidated slow taxis passed by with small plastic fixtures on their roofs, faultily lit. Behind us Sánchez's body or its covering lay sleeping or waiting.

Before going down the veranda steps and skirting the sculptural fountain, on my way to the street, I recalled the title of one of Sánchez's books, *Aire sobre el aire*, 'Air on the Air,' that title which defines his intangible vocation so well. And I realized that this was the feeling conveyed by his presence in life, an anxiety that could not be contained and thus looked to escape. In a way, Sánchez's polished skin reminded me of the surface of some of Baroni's images and, following that train of thought I imagined for a few moments that her figures didn't really seek to imitate living people, let's say, but to show the skin of the dead, as if they were presences of inert beings that had been propped upright. Now I'm looking again at that poem with the line that gives title to the above-mentioned book, where on the bottom half of page 29 it says: 'we, amused, compulsive, tragic / we are pure crucible / word and understanding / – the heart of no one.' Sánchez's unusual emphasis, underscoring and refuting at once, was expressing that redundancy some objects need in order to be seen; for example, not air alone, but instead saying additionally air on the air. Once those objects were animated, Sánchez's intent, I thought, was to assign them a nostalgia; not so much of happiness or of a missed occasion but of inevitably incomplete experience. Later on I'll probably describe the effects of these strategies of emphasis, so to speak, on form as the impact Sánchez hoped his work would have.

The overwhelming presence of nature, as I said above, with its typical buzzing but with its gravity as well, weakened Baroni's voice still further. No particular category of noise – cicadas or the more or less distant barking of other dogs, very audible nonetheless, or the repeated laboring of a faraway motor – brought that effect about; it was instead the entire surround, which by virtue of the exact weather conditions and time of day, including the presence of the underlying sounds, not to mention the dominant scents at that moment, revealed itself as a deep crackling, a fairly slow murmur, which deigned to tolerate our presence but in return expressed itself as, let's say, a latent threat, one excessively on edge. So in Baroni's garden I verified once more that the supposed equilibrium of the wild seems instead like a final countdown; nature instills fear in us. And that despite its being a well-regulated nature, as I'll probably describe later on, though varied and profuse enough to display itself in keeping with the scale of the wild and, above all, to serve as a reminder or a warning of its original strength.

The garden parcel was surrounded by areas of un-cultivated growth, and at moments Baroni spoke of future expansions as if physical limits didn't exist and it were a question of a vast terrain belonging to her, endless, at least on two of the three visible sides. She would gesture toward something with her arm outstretched, and keep it raised while describing in her inaudible voice the flowering path she'd open up or the plantings intended for those corners; that's how she described the themes of future plots. In the region where Baroni lives, the backs of houses abut on open space; the impression is that the mountain ends there and each inhabitant can decide how to arrange that border according to whim or need. As you arrive, you notice instantly that Baroni's house is at the epicenter of an ever-expanding area, as I just said, where different notions of a garden nevertheless coexist. I'll probably describe this later on, but for now I'd like to point out that the idea of a profuse, even self-replicating, garden, one that nonetheless requires a human hand, Baroni's in this case, to spread and fulfill its purpose, let's say, whether soothing or shady, depending, also applies inside the house, invading floors and walls, and at times transforms it into something ambiguous, an anteroom to or longing for what grows outdoors.

When you go in, the first area you discover is given over to the display of Baroni's carved figures. It's an austere room like the rest of the house, and on the sky-blue walls you can see several vines painted with occasional flowers, their undulating stems arising from or putting out roots in the lower part of the wall, where they entwine; at times these garlands twist into single tendrils higher up on the wall, with, I think, a still more precious intent. Baroni has painted those vines outside the house, too, both on the exterior walls and on the columns fronting the veranda, also on several medium or large garden stones, and even in some corners that at first sight go unnoticed; vines otherwi.. identical to those on the 'tree' against which the woman on the cross is leaning, a few steps from where I am now. In the right-hand corner of the room that day were two tall Virgins, one green and another yellow, keeping an eye on the opposite corner with the habitual silence of their kind. To one side of them was the woman on the cross, smaller and of course much less ostentatious, her gaze lost in the same fixed point as always. Behind the wood carvings rose the vegetal- and floral-garlanded wall, as I said, and at eye level, in the center of the wall, a variety of pictures were hanging. Some were photos, the majority diplomas or commendations, and there were a few strictly decorative or commemorative paintings of a landscape or a religious figure; apart from that, on one tiny shelf or another there were a few decorative or personal objects, most likely endearing. There was another wall, off to the side, small and set apart by a beam, that held a greater number of pictures and diplomas. I began examining the diplomas, many of them had that decorative, sometimes vividly colored trim that makes the written testimonial stand out, and I noticed that the entire wall of this room was similarly arranged, with painted vines surrounding the central area, where the diplomas were.

The newcomer felt the impact of this austere atmosphere, which despite the many signs of the outdoors represented a space that was too empty and for long stretches of time, one might suppose, maybe often forgotten. Yet it revealed more than its stripped-down state promised, because in its economy (the few objects, but also the handful of decorative motifs that were nonetheless repetitive enough, the vacant corners) it exposed Baroni's delicate situation, planted between nature and art, on the one hand, and between permanence and transience on the other. Even what little of the house that I additionally managed to see later confirmed for me the impression of encountering something brief or provisional, ready to quit the premises in a few hours and in that case to leave behind traces of the recent occupants that, however well-defined, were at the same time completely mute, or rather, suddenly silenced. Yet this wasn't a mere attribute of the house, I think, but instead a quality united to the objects Baroni makes, meaningful and mute at once, eloquent and inexpressive.

Perhaps owing to that stripped-down atmosphere, in which everything was conceived for contemplation and in some cases, depending on the object, for worship or celebration (the wood carvings, the small religious prints, the painted garlands), one immediately felt cloistered, or out of place, despite being surrounded by a great deal of unoccupied space. The emptiness became more obvious because of the ornamentation, which absorbed the attention, great or small, that one might have. That attention would come back to anyone at all, to me in this case, as intrigue or bewilderment, because a struggle was being staged between different ways of seeing. The visitor would then receive contradictory signs, some arising from the idea of a museum or gallery (the display of the artworks) and others from the image of scarcity represented in that room with no furniture.

I stood in silence for a while, amid the artworks and the walls. The smallest frames contained honorable mentions of the most varied sort, but all done in calligraphy; at times Baroni would make a comment to me about this diploma or that; she was proud of every one of them. At a certain point I noticed that she had left, I hadn't realized it at the time, but in the end I saw her come in with a book in her hand, a few pages long. As far as I know, it's the only one she's written to date; it's called *Message of Love*. I began to look through it; on the cover you could see an angel garbed in yellow, flanked by blue and white wings and two parrots perched on flowering branches. I now have the copy at hand and every so often I reread it, as I might describe later on, though I'm not sure.

Thinking perhaps of resuming the tour, once she'd finished talking about the book Baroni said, 'Here's my workshop,' or something like that, and headed toward the left-hand side of the room. She proceeded with short steps, tired and hurried at once, her shoulders leaning forward as if she wanted to arrive quickly, most likely pushed onward by some uneasiness. Though she was convalescent her movements seemed urgent; so that I wondered if that manner, or inclination, wouldn't reveal a condition difficult to control and which led her to move in a somewhat disjointed way; taking weary steps because of her illness, yet faithful to her body's involuntary habits. I was also struck by a sort of eagerness or pressing need on Baroni's part to seek in her interlocutor some confirmation regarding what she said or did. This became more conspicuous to me when I saw much later, in a museum screening room, a documentary filmed in her house, where she needed to confirm the good or bad tenor of her answers in the interviewer's reactions. But it would be an exaggeration to say it like that, first of all because Baroni isn't an insecure person; on the contrary, I've known few people of stronger and more lasting convictions. As I observed her gestures in the film I relived several things I'd noticed on my visit, and it all made me reflect that perhaps that pleasantness or dependency on her interlocutor's mood came from the dramatic circumstances of her past, on the one hand, and from being an artist of humble origins, on the other.

Then, somewhat abruptly, Baroni opened the door that led to the workshop, and we entered a long, narrow room with windows facing the front of the house and one of its sides. I should say that she didn't actually open any door, she simply had me go in. But in doing so she made a gesture of such simple theatricality that I felt I was stepping onstage, as if she had effectively opened the way with a practiced protocol, or better, as if Baroni had revealed to me a secret entrance, indistinguishable in the room's dimness, beyond which the true action would begin. Behind us we had the rest of the audience, made up of the two Virgins and the woman on the cross. That's not entirely how it was, however. It seemed more like a frozen stage set. In the workshop I saw first of all how the signs of manual, even physical, labor stood out; for instance, the tools and the tree roots or odds and ends of wood in various sizes. But I could also see her work had been sporadic, at least in this most recent and perhaps prolonged interval.

I stood like that, observing and making a mental note of my impressions, most likely mistaken, when Baroni seemed to read my thoughts. She spread her arms wide, wanting to take in the whole workshop, to explain inaudibly that lately, because of her illness, she hadn't been able to work on a regular basis. There was no need for her to tell me, I saw it, but from that moment and for the rest of the day I no longer anticipated her words, or her silent expressions and gestures either, which would instantly assert themselves without my realizing it. One could attribute the change in atmosphere to inactivity; not an air of abandonment, but rather of a sudden and unexpectedly prolonged absence. A similar layer of dust blanketed objects and corners without distinguishing between the closest and the farthest off. Here were the tools, waiting in the same random spot where the unfinished job had decreed they be left, the pieces that were half-done and yet a bit aged, etc. I imagined that without much effort an attentive gaze could reconstruct the unfinished tasks. But of course, not as much what was still to be done as what had been done already.

Pieces of wood were spread out in different corners, some of a considerable size, thick stumps or logs, as Baroni calls them, from old and, I suppose, worthy trees, and there were several more or less twisted giant roots, giant, that is, given the dimensions of the space, and there were also some thin laths, much like ornamental molding. Apart from that one could see a number of items, now difficult for me to pin down, and which I remember as occupied spaces and fluctuating shadows, I'd say almost interchangeable. Boxes of different sizes or piles of things, objects stacked and hidden in the semi-darkness of the place. Otherwise, and also I'm unaware of the reason, the tools seemed to me, the visible ones at least, scarcer than I would have expected and also rudimentary, hardly specialized or specific, and above

all I was impressed, though I don't know why, maybe
because of the contrast with the few hand tools, I was
impressed by the great quantity there was of brushes and
tubes of paint, of small jars, tins or containers for mixing
pigments, I suppose, and wooden boards or surfaces
of all sorts of materials on which to try them out. And
lastly, as I said, I saw a good number of half-made figures;
not only unfinished, but discontinued as well, hardly
blocked out and, one noticed, abandoned far longer than
had been originally foreseen.

Sánchez was a nocturnal and taciturn creature, and
there was a time when he'd call at night with the idea
of having a conversation. The phone would ring and I
knew it would be him; that's why before answering I'd
prepare something to have on hand, for example a glass
and something to drink. On the other end of the phone
he'd be drinking as well. We could talk for quite a while,
though it depended on the occasion. I would be hearing
the noises on my street, I couldn't close the windows
because of the heat, and would notice that Sánchez, in
contrast, was surrounded by a deathlike silence; even
the echo of his own voice was perceptible, as if he were
speaking from an empty room. He was without doubt
ensconced on the sofa he used for resting and reading,
with his bottle, his glass, his notepad, his pile of books,
and his cigarettes, too. Malena was most likely reading
or working in another room on her translations. And
meanwhile the entire city surrounded Sánchez beyond
those walls with its nocturnal and verdant buzz. He
had an agility all his own for going from specific and
domestic matters to general and abstract issues, which
he typically used to clinch an argument and as a possible
example for the other topics. Moreover, he tended to talk
about himself; not as an exercise in vanity, something
foreign to his nature (Sánchez was a nostalgic creature,
too, and because of that his only conceivable vanity

was that of referring to his past, though with overtones of gratitude for what he'd experienced), but rather as a concern and even a complaint in the face of the passage of time and, especially, solitude.

A constant reference was his papers, to which he gave little importance despite his friends' exhortations to publish them; his papers with poems in manuscript, which he had, without exception, memorized. Regarding his manuscripts, difficult conversations might arise that ended in a decidedly gloomy fashion, because Sánchez was a writer uninterested in publication and even less in the various rites of literary circulation; advancing age, however, had confronted him with the fleeting nature of one's own existence, let's say, and with the inevitable conciseness of his work compared with the expansiveness of the future. He feared publication because of the errors that might slip in at the printer's, he'd say, and because it also caused the poem to coagulate, though a long time might have passed since he regarded it as finished. The ideal poetry was made up of mental poems, free of any physical concession. Likewise, I thought I noticed that he was subject to a very personal dilemma, the result of his anxiety at discovering that he hoped for recognition, something that had only recently become necessary to him, in contrast to his literary and even ethical beliefs, which led him to be suspicious of literary institutions and their related ups and downs: like success, failure, publication, ostracism, etc. Then I imagined him alone in his darkened room, surrounded by a tranquility that even he might consider excessive.

The truth is we saw each other face to face on very few occasions; strictly speaking, ours was a phone friendship, even if a bit irregular at that. He had bitter memories of his youth. He also felt a generic and more or less habitual remorse that led him to acknowledge, apologetically,

that in his lifetime he'd been much too irascible, and that
at times that temperament of his recurred persistently.
A long-standing regret, from his student days, was linked
to his father, who had repeatedly implored him not to
abandon his studies. The young Sánchez did not obey
him and left the university. Nonetheless, from that point
on his father's letters would be addressed to 'Professor
Juan Sánchez Peláez.' Sarcasm, invective or consolation,
Sánchez would never know, but it was all the same to
him. Once a certain moment in our conversation had
arrived, his voice would enter a state of exaltation. That
was my name for the point at which, because of the topic,
the alcohol, or the degree of intensity that had built
up, Sánchez's emphasis would reach such a pitch that it
verged, at times, on rage. At any rate, peace always arrived
quickly and instantaneously. Sánchez wrote in a poem:
'Like radiance or foliage / and over the fountain
of the murmuring garden / I am dead and I live / alive
and dead at once. / Without lamentation. / With an
almost absurd patience / I live / walled-up or hidden /
free / dead.' In another poem from his, as we can see,
funereal cycle, erratic as it is, he wrote: 'If it were up to
me / on concluding my cycle and my / allotted time /
I'd be alone / calm / the morning and the dawn / would
be awake / So / as I go by / as I pass through / dead /
the light will be moved / – by leaf and tree.'

I've put down these lines of Sánchez's and I'm not quite
sure why, beyond natural admiration. Homage and
recognition, obviously. I find no better way to make
certain lines my own than by copying them, adding them
to the more or less continuous flow of what, for good
or ill, is in me to say. Almost the same weakness I have
before Baroni's figures, which are especially suggestive
while saying the minimum. On several occasions Sánchez
was denounced or extolled as a surrealist; at other times
his confessional style and subjectivity were praised.

What I take away is that he is among the few who, in his day, did not weave an idyll out of the nature of the provinces but rather out of the natural motifs of cities. Gardens, fountains, trees, shade. At times one might think Sánchez's nostalgia is a nostalgia for *modernismo* – to whose set design he remained surprisingly faithful, like a permanent joke – in different garb.

I was walking away from the place where they were holding the vigil and was already on the avenue of the giant trees, actually a short distance from where Sánchez had lived during his last years, when an impulse prompted me to go back. Only a few minutes had passed, everything remained the same. The poet's friends received me effusively, like the member who returns to the clan after ascertaining there's nothing worthwhile out there; and I hadn't even reached them before they were offering me a new plastic cup. I excused myself and headed on to the empty chapel, empty except for Sánchez. In the midst of the silence the muffled laughter of the women in the group reached us; that laughter seemed a bit nervous and a bit defiant, as in Italian movies from the years when Sánchez, I think, had been young. Once beside the body I didn't know what to do. Nothing had changed, at least nothing visible, and each thing within that space seemed to keep to its own course, independent of what might be happening outside. I was studying Sánchez's safari jacket, I was impressed by its fit, how well it looked on him, as I said above, when one of his friends came in and began to recite the poet's lines. The tiger licks its jowls, or its flank, I recall his saying. It was the soldier's song, the paying of last respects.

At that moment I began to think, probably influenced by this chain of events, of several people I knew who were not at the funeral home that night despite being friends of Sánchez's. I set myself the condition that I'd consider

only those whose home address I knew. Thus someone
who lived a scant hundred meters from the place came
to mind; another who lived some eight hundred meters
away; a few additional people at different distances. Then
I tried to imagine what they would be doing; almost
all of them would be sleeping, I supposed. And lastly, I
mentally sketched a star over the map represented by the
territory. The center was Sánchez, the funeral home, and
each ray went to the house, even up to the bed, of each
of these friends. The result was an exceedingly irregular
diagram, but that wasn't the important thing. I told myself
that for a fraction of time the drawing presented Sánchez
as the heart of the city. A self-abnegating heart, of course,
since it was surrounded by silence and indifference. That
was how in a brief while I left the funeral home twice.
The friend of Sánchez's who drew near to recite also came
in to watch me, probably, I thought, sent by the others
because of my unexpected return.

In the workshop there were practically no decorations,
in contrast to the room by the front door. Here Baroni
had decided to cut herself off from the vegetal landscapes
on the walls and from the finished works, so that she
could be alone with those that were embryonic, imagined,
or incomplete. Given these signs of absence, it surprised
me that Baroni's entrance had an immediate effect
of turmoil, as if silence and motionlessness had been
redeemed on the spot, translated into an inclination,
into a sort of friendliness toward her on the part of the
objects. I recalled those cartoon series for children, in
which inert but always useful things, utensils and tools
in general (plates, spoons, pencils or pitchers), took on
life and human behavior and began to sing and dance,
ready to start on some task, displaying their solidarity
with the work of people. In this sense, I thought, Baroni
also created intermediate beings, relatives of those
dancing figures.

It was at that moment of confusion, as I was pondering the ideas of abandonment and of activity (for a moment I fantasized I'd discovered a secret in this situation, a sort of ideal attained, although attained in a natural way, an ideal I might have sought for a long time, without success of course, and was now seeing achieved, bitter over its belatedness, but it was tangible at last); anyway, it was at that moment of confusion that Rogelio appeared, emerging from the depths of the workshop, most likely through a door concealed in so much semi-darkness. In Baroni's life there have been various saviors, one of them being Rogelio, perhaps the only person who fits that category, ever since he literally picked her up and offered to help her when she was on the run from her parents' house, after abandoning her young children and hiding out in the cemetery of Boconó. As I'll probably explain later, Baroni spent several days there, sleeping among the tombs. People began to notice her and christened her, since she wasn't known in the area, in keeping with her new abode. They also accused her of desecrating graves and went after her for that reason. In reality, Baroni had nowhere to live, but she'd established a more routine connection with death than anyone in Boconó could have supposed. Some time after those days in the graveyard, Rogelio appeared. It's likely that in the cemetery she found a tranquility not only denied her by her family, but abolished ages before from the past, present or future of her simple existence. For as one can understand, Baroni's was a life that didn't demand too much; and yet the little it asked for was in the end denied. As she says to anyone who wants to listen, and as I could confirm on seeing a documentary, Baroni decided to leave her children in the care of her mother and sister for fear of doing them harm, nor did she rule out being capable of killing them, so awful were the attacks of despair that made her weep without end or consolation.

Rogelio paused in front of us and Baroni spoke in her
thin whisper, of which I understood nothing, except
for what was predictable, perhaps, the fact that she
was introducing us. There was a ceremonial moment
and Rogelio said some sociable words, few in number
and probably infrequent, I thought, given the effort
he was making to overcome his reserve. In that area
around Baroni's house, and also in that town and in
the neighboring cities and villages, I'd almost say in
the whole winding land of Trujillo state and the other
Andean states, Táchira and Mérida, everyone I met up
with always proved reticent; or at least seemed subject to
a kind of reserve that consigned people to a language of
measured gestures and half-spoken words, from which
they were clearly reluctant to depart. At most, someone
might seek out a greater communication, and in that
case would attempt another sort of dialogue, but sooner
or later there would be a relapse (a sort of reality check)
and the person who had been so bold as to say those not
absolutely necessary words would in the end be defeated
by some secret qualm or an unpleasant association, I
don't know, and would then retreat, would resume the
usual flow, saying only what was essential, it was a sort
of verbal restraint, almost always looking down at the
floor, a gesture that also meant taking back what had
been said up until then with limited talkativeness. And
whenever someone departed from that behavior, it was
because they did not belong to this local world, to the
district. By what they say, it's the Andean temperament,
the influence of the elevation, the desolation of the high
plains, etc. Whatever the case, Baroni would thus be
an exception, maybe the only one in that vast territory.
At one point, during the brief exchange with Rogelio,
Baroni stepped a few meters away and, behind our backs,
began coughing over and over again. I hadn't realized it
before, it was only on rehearing her cough and watching
her body shuddering that I became aware of this woman's

weak constitution, similar in its fragility to the little sticks or small staves she had scattered about or bundled in the corners of the workshop, with an equilibrium at the mercy of the slightest movement or any breath of air, and which often embellish her figures by forming cloaks or dresses that seem, and only seem, to be movable. In reality, this respiratory ailment was a small thing if one compared it with other episodes in the troubled history of her health.

I said goodbye to Baroni before mid-afternoon. At that hour the temperature still, or once again, appeared to make things quiver. Those spells of intense heat which lead one to trot out descriptions of hazy outlines, refractions of light, objects in slow motion, etc. Yet I was struck by the inverse, speed; as if the temperature, exerting some form of terror, had a disintegrating effect and reality itself, in its multiple articulations, had been startled and wanted to flee from this situation immediately. You'd hardly gone out to the garden, and without even taking the first step or feeling the impact of the heat yet, you would already notice the anxiety, nature, at once free-flowing and crushed. You'd know that beneath that stillness a combustion was throbbing in which all the elements took part, and which revealed itself through isolated and spontaneous reactions. The smell of the mangos embedded in the ground, clearer than before, saturated the air, making them indivisible from the presence of any object in particular. I walked the thirty meters to the entrance gate, once more crossing through the distinct areas of the front garden, the oldest of them already established and dominating their sites, I mean proving less attention-grabbing, the novelty having adapted itself to the space, and I went out to the street, where I was naturally struck by the minimal difference between inside and outside, an irrelevant nuance, one could take that portion of the street to be the prelude or the coda to Baroni's garden. But of course, the same could perhaps be said of any space neighboring this property. Some years ago, the municipality of Betijoque baptized that street with Baroni's name, as a way of paying homage to its most illustrious figure. And yet there is little else that I remember about this almost deserted lane, as if beyond its probable lack of distinction, only the house, first, and the street name, second, would absorb the visitor's complete curiosity. The rest of the streets in Betijoque were empty as well. It was the moment for my return trip, I could have taken the quickest route, but I preferred to go back to Boconó taking the long way around, so as to acquaint myself with the western part of that territory.

At that hour Betijoque had lost the peaceful bustle of midday. No buses or cars could be seen, the stores were closed. A solitary person might appear, walking slowly, only to instantly vanish from view at the first corner. At that moment the avenue seemed excessively broad to me, I thought the desolation highlighted dimensions that at first glance were unnecessary. I don't know how to put it, the avenue demonstrated itself to be an obsolete and disused artifact, a deserted esplanade that was only the memory of what before and after Betijoque recovered its typical highway breadth. The façades of the houses, of the same concrete-gray as sidewalks and pavement, along with the gentle sloping of the terrain, brightened the transparent light of the highlands. In any case a few minutes later, after a three-block stretch, this principal avenue petered out near the town limit, to turn once again into highway, the road of the outlying area. The contrast between city and country is always spoken of. The emptiness, the density, the prolonged uncertain border. Yet on leaving Betijoque that afternoon I was struck by another type of contrast, which at that moment I experienced as more obvious and definitive because it was lacking in nuances. It was radical, like turning a page; in a minuscule fraction of time one was already surrounded by silence and nature. In this way, almost without realizing it, I found myself once again surrounded by the vast elevations, which revealed themselves by turns, whether one looked behind or looked ahead.

The road proved to be of dirt for nearly its entire length; there were sections, now impassable, that had been paved long ago, and others in better shape, especially when reaching a destination. While going up or down (for which the road etched a permanent zigzag on the slopes), or while proceeding through the winding area of the valleys (which followed the watercourses), one had the impression of being close to something that in reality was beyond the immediate surroundings, at an insuperable distance – the mountains, various and overlapping. What was distant drew closer perhaps owing to a purely visual effect, to the clearness of the air or to the uneven height and depth of the different elements of the landscape, whose relative positions were always in flux. The afternoon had clouded over. At times I drove into areas of low-lying clouds, where an incandescent cloudiness hid everything; banks of mist, thicker or less so, in the process of disintegrating. Without it raining, or through a rain made up of air saturated with dew, one discovered that all things, even the sheltered ones, were soaked and were dripping.

Every now and then there would be a break in the clouds, and through a breach in the peaks I could see the sun, peering out only to hide immediately behind another mountain or another cloud. I'd already read somewhere about the condensation effect produced by the region's arbitrary orography, which traps hot air inside the mountainous perimeter. I kept on leaving behind dormant hamlets, places where everyone seemed

to have retreated indoors or moved away. I came across
no other vehicle, and since at times the track of the
highway would disappear or overlap with the rocky bed
of a watercourse, or turn into a hardly visible trace that
was difficult to verify, I occasionally wondered if I were
really still on the route and if I might not be advancing
without any kind of route at all. At those moments one
could take any direction, with nothing to obey. It was
this thought about the chance nature of the road that
led me to think about chance in general, its ineffable
combination of destiny and causality, and about the
complicated matter of having met Baroni. Not the
circumstances that had made me seek her out and meet
with her, but about the influence, at that point unknown,
that meeting her would in the future have on me.

As I said, I met up with no other vehicles on the road;
throughout my life I've been in such situations far
too often: empty streets, inhospitable highways, an
abandoned world, as if all machines had declined
to participate. To this day I have no idea what this
recurrence means, perhaps that very little can be
rescued, variety is at first glance a desert lacking in
elements, and despite every effort, no quantity of will
can supply what reality itself withholds. Nonetheless
I came across a fair number of people on foot, far
from any visible town, who stopped with a curious
and cautious look on their face. If the entire region
seemed rural, as it is in fact, the drive that afternoon
underscored the difficulty inherent in any label, because
it was a district about to leave behind whatever it
had been in the past, a very available territory, whose
only tangible essence was solitude, as if nature itself
hesitated to make a definitive display and adopt any
alternative to random chance. On the gentle slopes of
the mountains one could occasionally see an isolated
pair of cows to one side of a small planted field. It is

one of the things that most attract one's attention in this region: the sparsely inhabited landscape, on the one hand, and on the other the constant signs of human labor. The houses and outbuildings are hidden under tropical growth, beyond the depths of ravines, on hillsides or atop plateaus or in barely accessible terrain, out of sight. And when one could manage to glimpse some dwelling, I realized a short time later, one would be absorbed by the strange combination of the façades' beauty and obsolescence. The shades of green call for a separate mention. The various gradations filled the entire landscape to overflowing, even the most distant heights, when the exact but darkened green of an escarpment would blurrily emerge, near-gray or near-black, among the clouds.

So as I was driving from Betijoque through that capricious landscape, I was thinking of Baroni's workshop, of the immobile figures in the gallery, and of the several others that were half-finished, in distinct stages of completion, but to which she'd referred as if they were already alive and all that was left to do was dress them, to bedeck them in a bright and colorful garb. When I got to Boconó it had already been dark for a while. Near the city, after one has passed through some towns I may mention later on, the road becomes more drivable; and indeed in the final stages the route followed the river on both banks at a varying remove, crossing it a number of times over rudimentary bridges. This river, moreover, has the same name as the city. In that land of imposing mountains (imposing not so much because of their size as because of the crazy overlap they've achieved), traveling by night, as opposed to day, is a trip through the darkness with no glimmers or degrees of depth. What little can be made out in the sky, if by providential luck it is faintly illuminated, is so directly overhead that you have the sense of traveling

at the bottom of a well, on the insuperable depth of
a depression. I could hardly imagine the firmament,
whimsically serrated by the mountains that surrounded
me at that moment. One could intuit at a vague distance
the masses of irregular bulks, and that turned the drive
into a flight through a single interminable shadow. This
impression became still stronger when I looked in the
rearview mirror and saw that the machine I was traveling
in was giving off pure darkness, nothing else, just like an
insatiable mouth that was pursuing me, only to expel me,
because I kept leaving it behind, upon another darkness,
blacker than any I'd known before.

In those moments of nocturnal passage, I thought also
that I'd turned into a denizen of solitude. Put like that,
it sounds a little affected or confessional, also pretty
lightweight; all the same, I was referring to something
practical. My conversations with others were becoming
more and more infrequent, in a rapid and apparently
uncheckable decline. I found nothing to say, hardly ever,
and what I heard always seemed insufficient to me. On
the one hand, my experience was increasingly limited, I
devoted ever longer periods just to thinking, to scattered,
free-floating lucubrations that were remote from any aim
or focus; and on the other hand, I realized that every day
I was more indecisive in my assertions, so much so that
I made distorted, untenable or downright unconvincing
comments, and anyhow that didn't matter to me
because I thought that the truth – whatever this was – as
pertaining to me would be found in the depths (not inner
depths, something I obviously couldn't believe in and
that perhaps no longer existed, but rather, in the depth
of things, that is, in the putative ultimate meaning of my
words). I was ruminating on these ideas among those
dark roads, noticing how mute, blackened nature was
in harmony with my thoughts and provided a backdrop
for them. I imagined that those valleys with their

hidden population were the only territory in the world
I was fated to live in; that I spoke with the intention
of making myself heard, but in a displaced language,
neither incorrect nor foreign, only distorted by the
conditions of the milieu, as if my voice were broadcasting
at a supernatural frequency; thus not only language
separated me from everything, also spatial coordinates,
the ever more restricted physical world, etc. At my age,
I thought in the midst of the dark mountain, at my age
I'm whining like a lonely little boy, etc.

Here to rescue me from these bitter sensations was,
first, the memory of Baroni and, second, the image of
her most dauntless figure, the woman on the cross.
Amid the dismal thoughts of the journey, that simple
woman of wood, attached forever to her destiny and
her attributes, emerged as the symbol of wise and
muted resistance. Muted not like my silence, which was
timid and neglectful, but muted like understanding
and comprehension when they don't bother to learn
what every single thing is about. I, the individual who
understands nothing and wallows in his limitations,
and she, the image (person, scene or representation)
who understands everything. I had a foreboding
of her inert body at my back, indeed a good many
kilometers ago and a number of geographical obstacles
far behind, and quite the opposite of any abstract or
esthetic presence, I felt her as a figure who soaked up
experience, sublimated it; I felt that, whatever happened,
she would understand everything. In this way, the
mystical predisposition revealed itself, in all likelihood
despite Baroni's intentions, as a profoundly practical
attitude, capable of encompassing any aspect of or turn
of events, however unique the case might be, like my
own and my situation and meditations under those
circumstances. I imagined the past of the woman on
the cross, a childhood given to dreaming in the heart

of the countryside, a brief and troubled youth, a
disastrous and premature adulthood; it was myself,
to be exact, incapable of describing myself under any
circumstance with some guarantee of reliability.

Of course I couldn't make any clear deductions; an
unconnected sequence of premises and episodes of a
different nature complicated every approach. I could
obviously invent something, assign a possible past to
the woman on the cross, perhaps pretty close to Baroni's
real one. Nonetheless any description of the facts
would be only halfway comprehensible and in great
part entirely indecipherable. For certain things fiction
wasn't any good; I'd always suspected this, but now it
was absolutely clear. And why wasn't it? Not because
it distorted the truth, that could be praiseworthy, but
because it revealed itself to be a useless trick. I couldn't
imagine who would be interested in the past of a wooden
figure, even if I happened to present her as somebody
real. But interested wasn't the word: who would be
inspired by it to some feeling, to at least an affinity,
or be afforded some lesson, when we all know that life
hides no secrets. Baroni had overcome the obstacles and
barriers to making a symbol capable of radiating life,
shall we say, but inept at assimilating it or preaching it.

At that hour, when I arrived, Bocⁿó seemed an empty
city. The last river crossing had led me straight to the
hotel, where the few lit lanterns, but above all the
solitary, regular song of a cricket, watchful somewhere
in the trees, indicated the late hour. For some reason
I don't know, as soon as I went in the hotel room, the
cricket was no longer to be heard, as if it had stayed
up expressly for my coming while flaunting its song
of waiting. I went to bed without managing to sleep;
perhaps because of this, the next day I was struck by
the morning's presenting itself like any other while I,

who had not stopped thinking about the woman on the cross since my pessimistic meditations on the highway, was nevertheless perceiving the signal of something different, the parallel, or better, the foreign time in which the figure had installed me. Fantasy, tiredness or suggestibility, it was in any case something that distanced me from this particular day and at the same time put me back inside it, because I noticed the impact of what was new, the beginning, let's say, of a different time within the continuity of days. Something similar to what one feels in the face of the death or the birth of a loved one. One is likely to have spent long hours in the funeral home, the entire night or the whole day, and on coming out to the street is nevertheless going to notice the indifference with which reality endures the absence (Borges observed this as well), which throws us for a loop and points to reality, and in this way encloses us in it, to our surprise but more entirely than before, when that other person still occupied the air.

I think Baroni could endorse these impressions, if one takes into account that during her cataleptic experiences she saw, or pondered, the unfurling of reality as she faced her death. For example, at age eleven in her first attack, which lasted twenty-four hours, she was glad when her grandparents arrived at the wake, but was immediately saddened to realize they were going to bury her and so she couldn't be with them. The double gaze (the normal one, from the world of the living, and the constructed one, from the zone of death) fulfills the requirements of self-consciousness. This childhood episode had a lasting effect. At age thirty-three she suffered the second attack, this time for seventy-two hours. It took place at a moment of despair, when Baroni rolls down a ravine and is left unconscious. Since then, death had needed no tricks of catalepsy: Baroni began to portray her own death and in doing so formalized that double gaze, seeing herself through the eyes of those who have stayed alive, and offering to the living the lesson of seeing her dead.

Beyond this, that morning in Boconó had nothing special about it. As ever in this region of low mountains, the weather was a little chilly and, at that time of year, fairly dense clouds were flying by at low altitudes. During the night I had been witness to the continuous murmur of water, the flowing of the river ten meters from my window, which reached me like an activity separate from the world, perhaps originating in some barely living organism that had chosen that way of revealing itself. The river was the most obvious presence, at least until around three in the morning, when you began to hear, at first sporadically and a bit timidly, the birds. It may seem an exaggeration to say it like this, but as the night went on I could distinguish the most delicate sounds of that corner of the Earth. The city narrows the watercourse slightly, and there you can tell that the river is a bit more compressed: I was hearing the splashes dripping and the gentle turbulence against the banks and among the stones. There were moments when I didn't know whether the water had lulled me to sleep and I kept hearing it in a dream, until I would be awakened by the surprise of dreaming something that was happening at that instant, or whether my attention, being wide-awake, was filling in the half-sketched noise until it was whole, with the help of other memories of the kind, fountains, streams or waterfalls in general recognized from the past.

As I got into bed I had thought that the night would prove long; and indeed it did. I dozed at times, and on waking my first thoughts zeroed in on the woman on the cross. I saw her in an unfamiliar room, which nonetheless belonged to Baroni, in the company of the green Virgin and the other yellow one, both of course more sanctimonious and elegant, and I was thinking

that unlike her companions, the woman on the cross
had been sentenced to ostracism that went beyond
the austerity or abundance with which destiny might
surround her; she was the image of a devotion that had
not yet materialized, probably not even available. I was
startled at every moment and couldn't understand my
anxiety. I had given up trying to get the woman on the
cross out of my mind, I found that impossible; but I kept
thinking of her the way children yearn for the dolls they
love, with urgency and reverence. Later, if I dozed off
again, I would dream that the woman approached me
holding out her hand, which I would keep hold of for
the rest of the dream; only thanks to this help could I
rise from the bed, where for some unknown reason I
lay paralyzed, but it wasn't really the bed in the hotel in
Boconó, but instead a bed set up in the depths, at the
bottom of an especially deep well. It occurred to me
that that tunnel was the nocturnal drive from Betijoque
hours before; hence the dream meant that the woman on
the cross was rescuing me so that I could take her; in the
language of half-waking, so that I could recover her.

A few hours later, when the sun began to filter through
the curtains of the room, the woman on the cross was
still the silent and immoveable character, I'd say almost
insubstantial, on whom my thoughts were fixed. I got up
and opened the door of the room. The day was bright.
It was like coming across an enormous garden; I felt a
slightly goofy astonishment, innocently enough, before
nature so pristine and tranquil-looking. There were the
parking spaces, one for each room, and beyond them the
dense foliage of the trees, the paths that led to the area
with the cabins, and above the trees, at an indefinable
distance, the overlapping ridges of the mountains, to one
side, and to the other the city itself, built on steep streets
at that moment empty of cars, looking like narrow stone
esplanades. I didn't dawdle on my way out of the room

and at once, after crossing the river, I found myself
walking through those very lanes, the center of town,
where the shops were open despite the early hour.
Standing on street corners were old men of varying
types, or little old ladies, who seemed to make up a part
of the daily landscape in Boconó, who came from nearby
places probably hidden away in the mountains. That's
why I saw them getting out of jeeps, in many cases with
difficulty; these vehicles serve as public transport in the
steep areas. At one point on my walk, as I was coming
around a corner I saw an old man take a spill as he got
out of one; it happened at the other end of the block
and there were no people nearby to help him. I saw
how he got up slowly and then hobbled on his way.
I spent one or two hours walking around the center
like this, so that I toured through it several times. By
now people of all ages were getting out of the jeeps.
And so, a little bored by those fairly uniform blocks,
and particularly anxious, thinking all along about
the woman on the cross, I went back to the hotel to
attempt to speak with Baroni. I regretted having been
unresponsive to the piece, when the day before it would
have been easy to have asked its price and very probably
bought it and taken it away with me. But the impact
of the woman had been belated, or rather, delayed
and nocturnal, and it presented at first in the guise of
nostalgia, I don't know how to say it, the memory of the
figure as a simple and poignant entity, on the one hand,
but convoluted and enigmatic as well. I was sorry not
to be contemplating her at that very moment and was
gripped by the apprehension, probably unfounded, but
insistent, that some casual visitor, as I had been the day
before, would lay eyes on the piece and keep it.

Back at the hotel, I headed to the lobby, a room with
almost no furniture and where the few things on view
looked recently installed, or, conversely, about to be

moved out. A ceramic miniature in the shape of those Colombian buses known as *chivas*, with suitcases and fruit on its top, drew my attention because it was missing part of its hood, as if it had fallen down a ravine on an actual trip, and no doubt because there was nothing else at all on the long shelf attached to the wall. Now I think that here is where another of my habitual scenes took place; at hotel reception desks where I have very little to say and where out of thin air, or because of my clumsiness, embarrassing situations arise. In any event I asked to use the phone and steeled myself to make a call in front of the woman at the desk who, not far from where I stood, didn't stop looking at me. If talking with Baroni in person the day before hadn't been easy, doing so by phone could prove impossible. Aside from that, even as I searched for the number in my pockets I felt overcome by discouragement. My plans always got thinned down before they could begin to be realized, even though at the outset they had seemed fairly firm, more or less; all too soon what was left of them was a vague intentionality, in which I ended up floating on a sort of indifference. This would plunge me into contradictory states; and in general, it's something that keeps on happening to me. Let me explain; probably the decision to make the woman on the cross mine, though firm, contained its own limitation: my tendency to desert at the first obstacle, however secondary it might be. In this sense, the little or the great deal I needed to do (that depended on the specific circumstances) presented itself as approximately definitive. The simple material the piece was made of, its expendable character, and to a certain extent its happenstance existence, all of that seemed to demand my passivity, a kind of permanently lowered voice, even my consent to the slightest setback, not my steadfastness and still less a tenacity that would always seem inappropriate to me. In this way I would end up bowing to whatever was to happen with the least possible intervention on my part.

This hesitation led me, faced with the delayed response, to nearly hang up twice. I imagined the futile little bell in that deserted house and on the vast compound, and it magnified the sense of failure. Only the curiosity of the receptionist, who had noticed my urgency to place the call, kept me from breaking the connection. She had no work to do, that was clear, and so she followed my movements undisguisedly, with a natural familiarity and as if she were doing something obvious. When she had checked me in the day before, I'd been struck by her attitude, that state of being on the verge of asking something and holding back at the last moment, or of keeping quiet for a long time, though without ending the conversation. I don't know if she absented herself, or if it was I. Finally I'd been able to resolve the situation, not without some embarrassment from my point of view; putting an end to a dialogue that had wound up some time before. So while I began thinking of the best way to get out of this new snag, almost theatrical, with the receptionist its only audience, Rogelio's voice turned up on the line, answering with his customary discretion. He didn't ask me anything, he returned my greeting with a bare few words saying that Baroni was working in the garden and he would go call her. She was outlining paths, transplanting, deciding how to move the soil and imagining new thematic areas. I imagined a long time would go by before Rogelio found her in that great territory, and still more before Baroni put down her work and returned to the house.

As time went by, I thought I ought to say something or other to the receptionist as a way of lending some nuance to the wait. I turned my eyes to her, all set to start a conversation, and yet nothing occurred to me; at last I ended up smiling. Any possible remark seemed incongruous, pretentious, or circumstantial, beyond any response she might offer, always brief and perhaps also improbable as a response, owing to that business of the local reticence. However, the receptionist seemed to me a being so sheltered, a good part of the day in her at first glance solitary office, that my comments, I thought, would be directed not only at her but at the situation, would be like a dramatic flourish that the scene both called for and rejected. And that in the end discouraged me anew, nothing else; that my words could be interpreted as an action and not as words meant to pass the time.

I waited long enough on the phone. The reason behind the call was the woman on the cross, who had nonetheless moved temporarily onto a secondary plane; now first and foremost was getting to talk to Baroni, the owner, at any rate the creator and custodian of the piece. I proceeded to think about the relationship she establishes with her figures, and it occurred to me that she took them to be autonomous manifestations of only a few individual existences. According to Baroni's idea, there would be individuals capable of being replicated in infinite materializations, at times even divergent ones. The number of versions depends, in this case, on her, Baroni; on nobody else. The silence at that hour of the morning wasn't complete, but was instead rural (birds, with their songs less restrained than the ones at dawn, and also cars, muffled from the other side of the river), and the only thing I heard over the phone was a pulse every so often: the long-distance meter. By now I'd already ruled out chitchatting with the girl, and yet she was at times visibly intrigued, not overly curious but instead depending on me to say something, even if it was into the phone, making visible, in fact, her own theatrical bent.

I still had in hand, now needlessly, the piece of paper with Baroni's number on it, and I recalled the confusion of the previous afternoon writing it down, for I'd had a hard time making out what she was saying and also because she had several times gotten confused over the sequence, dictating something else, or scrambling it with other phone numbers she was remembering. For example, some while back she had lent out her cell phone. She told me she now had another and that she got mixed up among those two numbers and her phone at home. She kept on receiving the bills for the old one, always low but never the minimum, but she hadn't decided to ask for its return because the other person, she assumed, needed it too. She had missed having the other device in the hospital, it had stored in it the numbers she had to have, but finally she'd ended up managing. Baroni did not lay it out exactly that way, neither did she tell me in any detail, but I surmised it according to her explanation.

Some minutes went by like this until I heard a movement at the other end of the line and an instant later (hesitancy, I supposed) the thin whisper I'd been waiting for turned up. As can be imagined, talking was difficult; I tended to raise my voice needlessly, as a reflex to her lack of voice. First, I learned that the woman on the cross remained in place; no one had taken her away. Afterward we came to an agreement about the rest. If I'd understood correctly, Baroni would bring her to Caracas, taking advantage of a trip that was planned for the coming months. Apparently the woman on the cross would be mine; I was pulling it off. I cast a distracted glance at the Colombian bus, making sure it had been present for the entire conversation. But, if I can say it like this, the truth is that I felt immediately uncertain and above all frustrated. I found the agreement too vague, to be finalized within an uncertain time limit and under circumstances in which anything at all could happen: Baroni wouldn't make the trip, someone would come to her house, as I had done, and offer her more money and she – having forgotten our agreement, or in a quandary between honoring an agreement or seizing the chance to sell that piece and then make another one – would understandably choose the second option. For me, the ideal world at that moment would consist of Baroni's immediately coming, despite her illness, with her green carving, a portable replica of her own self, or for some piece of luck, improbable but one I couldn't stop thinking about, to generate a providential traveler going straight from her house to Boconó, that same day or the very next morning. Nonetheless, I had to console myself and to realize that it was another of my baseless illusions; I had to leave the finalization, let's say, of the purchase open to chance.

Months later I met up with Baroni in the town of Hoyo de la Puerta, at the house of a friend of hers, named Olga, with whom she stays when she travels to Caracas. The previous day, while we were talking, Baroni had handed the phone to Olga so that she could give me the address and the directions for finding the house. In Venezuelan municipalities the street names tend to repeat themselves, at other times it's a matter of avenues and streets with the same name, or similar names that reference another person or circumstance (or the same person but with a different attribute, as can be the case with Bolívar). It can also happen that there are secondary streets, arterial appendages with no way out on the other side, called branches; in general these are numbered, though not always consecutively, or are differentiated by the word *bis*. The confusing nomenclature and the irregular topography thus require some referential aids: a tree, a certain stone painted for that purpose, a restaurant, a white house, some sign, etc. In this way Olga provided me with a fairly detailed route, which didn't save me from finding the place only after making several detours, which nonetheless would have been longer without her help.

I had the payment ready since the week before; it was a
good number of bills, at least that's how it seemed to me,
above all when I hefted them. Baroni hadn't accepted
a bank deposit, as I proposed when I called her from
Boconó (for me it was also a way of guaranteeing the
woman on the cross, so that she wouldn't sell her to
somebody else) and, according to our conversation weeks
earlier when we agreed to meet in Hoyo de la Puerta,
she didn't want a check, either. I didn't know her reasons
for avoiding banks, though I didn't find them hard to
imagine. So that day, after circling the area several times,
which I'll probably refer to later on, I reached Olga's house
by early afternoon. I was wearing the backpack with the
bankroll; bulky not so much because of the price of the
piece, though it wasn't insignificant (I'll refer to this later
on, I suppose), but because of the low denominations
of Venezuelan currency. (Here, too, I was experiencing
another repeating scene in my life: a sum of money
converted into a great quantity of paper, whose value,
gathered up in that fashion, seemed to me unreal, or still
more, completely extravagant.) I rang the doorbell and
waited. I felt I was carrying the material equivalent, and
because material abstract, of the woman on the cross, her
representation and simultaneously a kind of surrogate.
The bankroll came to represent the agreed-on value
for the transfer, it was something at once simple and
unheard of.

Opposite the house, some meters nearer the end of the
street, was a *cochinera*, as they call restaurants that serve
pork. The restaurant's sign on the highway had been
mentioned by Olga as a point of reference, though because
of some error or damage it pointed in the wrong direction.
Hoyo de la Puerta is to the south of Caracas and is known
for, among other things, its *cochineras* and its *conejeras*
– where they prepare rabbit. It's almost always families
or couples on an outing who visit these establishments,

or people who work in the area, and for the most part they are open-air terraces, with broad vistas over the landscape, facing the breeze from the mountainous spurs that make up almost all of this locality. The back of the house where I would see Baroni abutted on a deep ravine, beyond which you could see a series of continuous hillsides, with their harmonious heights and descents, laid out in differing degrees of depth within the verdant landscape of the whole. In several respects Hoyo de la Puerta is a thematic territory of Caracas, which recalls its small-town roots, on the one hand, and the preexisting wilderness in the valley where it was founded. Something of what this city was in the past, whether it inspires nostalgia or regret, wants to be recovered in Hoyo de la Puerta (or reencountered, discovered, or outright invented).

Now I occupied a vague point of that territory, of which this restaurant functioned as the local epicenter, I mean reduced epicenter, but at any rate the nucleus of something in particular. I put myself in the visitors' shoes and imagined that they'd taken their own routes in arriving there, as I myself had done, and I thought those tracks would remain marked on the surface for an indefinite time. But of course, I was unable to verify the marks. So I made for myself a mental representation of the area, similar to the diagram imagined on the occasion of Sánchez's wake, as if I had before me an aerial photograph or a simple map: you could make out part of Hoyo de la Puerta, with its houses, hillsides, roads, ravines and small farms, but chiefly you'd see the physical organization from directly overhead. People's routes to get to the cochinera would be in colors; these roads would go on converging until they met on the highway indicated by Olga, to then descend, all in a group, forming a very thick stripe, along the ancillary street where I now

found myself. I also thought that my trace would
come up marked as an unexpected coda, because the
observer would suppose my destination to have been
the restaurant but that at the last minute I went off to
an ordinary house, unmarked, I should say, situated
across the street and thirty or forty meters to the side.

Since it was a weekday and early in the afternoon, I
assumed the *cochinera* wouldn't have many customers.
There were in any case a fair number of cars along the
curb, and the music that came from there invaded the
block. The façade of the restaurant was white, with
two half-arched windows protected by black wrought-
iron bars (this was another of the orientational aids,
now I could confirm it). A young man watched over
the customers' cars from the doorway; when he saw
me he thought I was headed there, and began waving
a white napkin at me as a kind of greeting. I signaled
no with my hand and he sketched a goodbye, which
consisted of keeping his arm raised for a moment. I
went on looking for Olga's house, until I found it. It
was white, too, and apart from the restaurant music
in the background, I could hear a noise coming from
inside the house that, I thought, would probably be
deafening indoors. In fact, ringing the bell several
times was useless. It occurred to me to knock, but
I instantly had to do so harder. Meanwhile I heard
a motor that seemed to be moving, I guessed that it
was nearing and immediately drawing away from the
door. I suppose that at a certain point someone heard
the knocking, because the machine stopped and they
came to open the door. Afterward they'd tell me they
were renovating. It had been a long time since I'd seen
floor tiles being polished, and this machine seemed to
me to be especially noisy. For some unknown reason,
maybe because it would have been presumptuous,
I didn't let slip any comment about this.

At that moment I suddenly thought, it was a brief fraction of time, let's say a second, probably less, and really more than a thought it seemed a notion: I wondered whether those simple obstacles that kept appearing, slight delays, distractions or detours, might not be signs or tests, harmless and of uncertain importance, but put there by chance or destiny so as to impress me with promises of a twisted epic; so that I could later say, 'I went through this,' 'It wasn't so easy,' 'It couldn't have been worse,' or things like that. In reality, it was already difficult to describe the time I'd spent submerged in permanent confusion; or I could pin it down, but it was a feeling so ingrained that it was a cadence, or an inclination, assumed as natural, much like a chronic pain. That night on the Trujillo highway, returning from Betijoque, this feeling made its appearance for the first time. It was, however, a first time relatively, because I'd had it from way back and only on that occasion had it manifested itself. 'What to call it?' – that's what I asked myself as they were showing me into Olga's house, what to call that feeling of distance and detachment, in which a state of latent shock, contained and thus sporadic, was mixed with a situation of despondency and daily confusion.

There were places in the house through which one could not pass. After negotiating several obstacles I reached the terrace, in the back, from which you could see the verdant hillsides of Hoyo de la Puerta, sprinkled with houses that looked like white or red grains of sand amid the greenery. I found Baroni comfortably settled in a rocking chair, attired in a multicolored dress that made her smaller, I'd almost say minuscule. And a few meters away from her, on a cement table studded with shiny stones, the bundle of paper and plastic bags sat waiting: it was the woman on the cross, protected by her traveling outfit. Baroni's legs still ached from carrying her on her lap during the journey, since she hadn't

wanted to check her as baggage. I explained above that
she prefers to call her crucified, the crucified woman.
She spoke of the woman as if she were somebody living,
but recognizing in her, at the same time, an obligatory
passivity and a complete indifference, the same as an
inorganic being's. Like the rest of Baroni's figures, the
woman on the cross radiated presence, which made
her immediacy inescapable. For Baroni, I think, that
immediacy translated into an aura of intangible but self-
evident life, which could be perceived at all times, even
in the deepest darkness, and it translated as well into the
special treatment she bestowed on each of her figures, as
if they were living dolls. The proof is that I myself could
immediately verify that presence, which made itself
apparent despite the paper and plastic that enveloped her
like a guarded and secret entity. In a few stages, which
nonetheless took time and required Baroni's help, pulling
off tape and removing bags, we unwrapped her.

'We'll set her here so she can look out at the mountains,'
Baroni said, placing her to face the hillsides that repeated
themselves to the horizon. It might sound a bit naïve,
but reencountering Baroni and the woman on the cross
moved me. Simply and suggestively, without being
heartrending. The woman on the cross not only consisted
of the piece of sculpted wood that was now confronting,
I suppose, the open space; she was also the silent figure
that I'd seen months before and that had acquired a
certain kind of added life during the wait and from a
distance. What kind of life? I don't know. Probably an
inert life, to the degree that it would be unverifiable
as organic for whoever wished to test it, and therefore,
most likely, a borrowed life; the loan as last resort.
The borrowed life would have a double component,
I thought. On one side is the person who created or
made the figure, in this case Baroni, and on the other
side should be someone who believes in some spiritual

component, no matter how minimal, of the piece. That person looked to be me. In my opinion, this belief has no obligatory religious connotation, although it could indeed be registered in the series of religious experiences that are offered to us by, let's say, modern life.

As I said before, the woman on the cross, despite her name or her sentence, is a laical being, in any case worldly as well. She's an infrequent phenomenon in Baroni's mostly religious work. Just seeing her, anyone would think of a young lady from a few decades back: she looks ready to go dancing, with her short rose-colored dress that ends in a slanting hem, a dancer's, baring more of the left thigh than of the right. She's wearing small boots, ankle-high, which thus show off her slim, well-shaped legs, joined at the knee and slightly bent to one side. It is in this arrangement of the legs, the body's large naked surface, where the figure's ambiguity is concentrated, for the posture refers as much to the decorous poses of the models as to the suffering immobility of those who have been crucified. That type of preparation for happiness, or for pleasure, of the whole ensemble, encounters an initial reversal in the woman's doleful air; she looks afflicted and gazes downward, as if casting a look of sorrows, like the saints. Then there are her hands, hidden behind her slim waist and presumably tied to the piece of wood where the girl has been fastened. Looking, then, at this woman absorbed in her sufferings before the majestic landscape of Hoyo de la Puerta, for her a stage set surely expressing nothing, it occurred to me that the wild sensuality of her body, somewhat innocent to the extent that it's a bit girlish, too, is the cause for the duress to which she finds herself subject. Yet at the same time the piece of wood that restrains her finds its justification in the woman's nature; without this contrariety, as it were, between carved wood and natural will, there would be no figure and no martyrdom either. I have to say that only then,

and after half-formulating these ideas, did I find in the
two of them, person and figure (creator and carving),
an obvious resemblance. I'm not referring to their faces
or their hair, a likeness I've already mentioned that is
practically a solemn rule of Baroni's art, but instead to
their attitude, the feeling deposited in their expression.
It sounds a bit abstract, but it's what I mean.

I knew that when she was a very young girl, Baroni
had been forced by her parents to take up adult life
in a pretty brutal manner, handed over to the man who
would become her husband. That episode inaugurated
a long and difficult period, of suffering and doom that
motherhood didn't change or improve, or even soften,
but instead made worse. As Baroni tells it, she was in
love as a girl with a slightly older boy, with whom she
exchanged notes that they left under the stones of a path
on the outskirts of town. This boy was very poor; as
Baroni says, using her own habitual form of emphasis,
'He was poorer than poor.' She imagined being married
to him, but at the same time suffered when she thought
that, because of his poverty, they would only be able to
build a house with some sticks of jambu, a wood nearly
useless for that task. In any event, her parents betrothed
her to a man twenty-seven years her senior, at which her
secret love left town for good. When Baroni recounts
these episodes, it is as if she were reliving that confused
moment of guilt and spite, almost childlike and therefore
very enduring, with an astonishing attention to detail.
(Decades later she heard news of her young boyfriend
and went to visit him in the cemetery; he had died in a
nearby town.) I've seen a film in which Baroni evokes
him, precisely under that useless tree, a jambu, close to a
stream, at what amounts to a natural altar in his memory.

She suffers the first attacks of desperation some time after
her marriage; and when her emotional and psychological

state becomes unbearable, she abandons her husband and returns to her parents' home along with her children. But this doesn't help her, her parents subject her to a more intense regime of control and punishment than before. Baroni isn't asking for much, only a normal life. Then the crisis becomes more acute, desperation leads her to cry all the time. One day she abandons the paternal home with what she has on, leaves her children, whom she feared she would kill in an attack of madness, under the care of her mother and sister, and sets off on the local roads with no exact destination. Seen in retrospect, the flight was the beginning of the solution. After a journey of several days on state highways, she arrives in Boconó, attracted by the city's name, which she considers auspicious, to end up settling temporarily in the cemetery.

Thus, it occurred to me to expect traces of that sad past time in the woman on the cross: youth extinguished, femininity imprisoned and the body under the yoke. In Baroni's artistic imagination, the woman on the cross is present as a perpetual condition, which has not concluded. One part of the figure refers to the past; rather, to two pasts: Baroni's own, as a captive woman, and the artificial one, to give it a name, belonging to the wooden figure's hypothetical history, that is, the moment, perhaps impossible to pinpoint, when Baroni decides to create the image, when it 'appears' in front of her, before its existence proper, as if it were an action or a word to be carried out but not yet complete. And another part of the woman on the cross refers to the future, in this sense it is like any work of art, because, once finished, it's placed in the realm of the contingent: it belongs to the world and submits to the passage of time. The lines that run through past and future of course have ties of continuity; but in that weaving the woman on the cross appears as a complex point where the flow of that

relationship is concentrated and slows down, because it
recapitulates the past, from which it fixes an image, and
it establishes the figure in relation to the future, though it
may be only a silent and even absent presence. A new start,
or better, the new start for a life already lived. Baroni's
past is brought up to date thanks to the work of art; she
is simultaneously settled more comfortably in the past, in
what was left behind, as if someone (Baroni or the woman
on the cross) had buried it and dug it up in a single action.

In the meantime, the floor polisher began to whirr once
more; it may have been running all along but I noticed
it again only now. A link with what had gone before and
what was to come, seen from various angles, the woman
on the cross also had the virtue of suspending the present
moment, the now, so to speak, and of taking us to a level
of diffuse presence, only halfway evident, as if it were a
matter of occupying an imperfect temporal plane, where
two dissimilar elements got jumbled together, nostalgia
and celebration. I took the money from the backpack
and handed it over to Baroni. And as was to happen
to me some months later, when I received the saintly
doctor from her, at this moment too it seemed to me an
inadequate amount. I don't know if by a lot or a little;
in any case it established a paradoxical relation with the
woman on the cross. The word 'buy' was the correct one,
nonetheless it designated a terse civil or commercial rite,
more incidental than real. On the one hand, I knew there
was no exact amount of money that summed up the value
of the piece; on the other, the idea of a changing of hands,
of ownership, was also shown to be wrong. I felt calmer
thinking of a species of loan, of ownership rights, of
guardianship (of custody, as Baroni had opted to do
with the first Virgin of the Mirror). At a future moment,
the woman on the cross would be back in Baroni's hands,
or she would go to a true owner, an incidental one, without
it mattering to whom she belonged.

On that other afternoon I began describing above, at her house in Betijoque, I had asked Baroni if she wouldn't want to make a saintly doctor for me. We're talking about the doctor who now spends his days in this room, a short distance from where I write, with the exemplary crack running down his middle. Rogelio took part in the conversation. I phrased the question cautiously, to avoid sounding presumptuous, because I recognized that other artisans refused to make the saintly doctor – or to make him again if they had done so already – or had decided outright never to make him at all. It's odd how the word most frequently used by those artists was, and I assume still is, 'to make'; it's not 'to carve,' 'to prepare,' 'to work' or another like it: it is innocent and demiurgic, it is 'to make' as if one said 'to construct' or 'to create.' In reality, it is making in the sense of swelling the ranks of what exists, of adding to the series a new individual. That the saintly doctor is anathema to several artists could be due to superstitions, promises or things of the kind, related to the religion or personal story of each one. I'm acquainted with artists who don't make the saintly doctor because they're very devoted to him and, as a result, fear him, they don't consider making him a means of glorifying him, just the opposite; and I'm acquainted with others who don't make him because they're not sufficiently devoted, and so fear wounding one of the saint's sensibilities. Luckily Baroni had no objections, on the contrary. It was hard for me to make out the answer in her muffled voice, but from her enthusiasm I inferred that she hadn't carved a doctor in quite a while and would be happy to make one again. Later on Rogelio courteously confirmed, though unemphatically, what Baroni had said.

In Rogelio one could easily find the Andean temperament I described above, I thought, as if we were dealing with a prototype. Attentive and at the same time quiet, he settled into situations without making his presence known; and as

a result, the things and the people around him, permeated
by Rogelio's reserve, also projected an atomized presence
into their surroundings, in many cases unnoticed. And
so not only he himself, even the atmosphere around
him tended toward weightlessness; not toward what
was unreal or indistinct, but instead toward what was
latent and devalued. Indeed, on numerous occasions it
would happen that you could shut out Rogelio's presence
without realizing it, when he would in fact be a few
meters away, generally off to one side, the least prominent
corner, toward which no one would look. And when
you discovered him you'd notice how his air of absence
was the opposite side of the penetration with which he
was following the event so as to draw, I suppose, his
own conclusions or lessons. That state of being attentive
without its being explicit was, on the other hand, the
drastic expression of an almost reverential courtesy that
always aligned itself with silence.

I'm going to give an example, or something close, of
Rogelio's watchful presence: when you're going into the
house where Baroni lives, after passing through the gate
on the street and then having walked a fair number of
meters through the front garden, you'll find several trees
decorated with drawings and paintings on their trunks.
Two of these trees present human silhouettes. One is
Rogelio, the other is Baroni. Naturally, the bodies adapt
their shape to the quirks of the tree; Baroni has taken
advantage of the first forking: both figures stretch their
arms upward. And in the trees' crotches, that is, between
their shoulders, she's placed egg-shaped boards on which
both faces are painted, one representing herself and the
other Rogelio. It is Rogelio, his arboreal manifestation
and his mask, a figure that lies between naïve painting
and childish caricature, who occupies the first visible tree
when you're coming in by way of the path from the street.
Baroni's image is to the left, several meters from Rogelio,

preceding another lateral section of the property that
I'll perhaps describe further on. In this way Baroni too,
I suppose, grants to Rogelio a protective role. In the end,
knowing the part he played in the rescue of the person
who would later be his wife, it's not something that strikes
one; taking her in when she was living in the cemetery
and surely looked like one of those half-clandestine
beings, also eccentric and wretched, who are the outcasts
of town, on the fringes for some reason, and tend to live
with their own tragedy where houses become few and
far between.

Rogelio's protective presence has been enduring ever
since and became evident during numerous vicissitudes;
nonetheless the drawing on the tree doesn't depict
him as a mere beneficent authority, but instead as a
childlike presence, a party to the game. A celebration
of coexistence and of nature, the painted trees seem
surrogates for the real people. They offer a surface, their
dark-colored bark, and faced with this setup (as another
artist might say, faced with the attraction or the challenge
of the canvas) Baroni colonizes them with the figures
of the people who live in the house. It may seem a bit
ingenuous as a proposal or artistic construct, but probably
what it seems like hasn't the slightest importance. I'm
not going to make the mistake of wondering if Baroni
is or isn't seeking an art of conceptual impact, or of a
conventional type, nor if she conceives her works as
pieces of conservation or of aesthetic exaltation. The truth
is that Baroni's premises interest me up to a certain point:
that point where her work becomes possible; certainly,
this ought to be true for all questions about the technical,
esthetic or moral presuppositions of artists.

I believe I referred earlier to Baroni's delight in decorating
the stones of her garden, the interior and exterior walls of
her house, I've just mentioned the tree-people, etc. I don't

know if this arises from some idea or disposition in favor
of a 'total art,' it seems to me instead that Baroni is subject
to two forces. One leads her to believe in representation,
the other impels her to seek ornamentation. These things
are not so far apart, at times they even complement each
other or get mixed together, it depends on the observer's
attitude, on the creator's intentions, on ideas in general
about the work, etc. But in Baroni ornamentation is related
to the aestheticizing touch, to embellishment, to praise
and natural exuberance; it is a sense that is unambiguous
and always straightforward, it is not a decadence or
a concession. Beauty coincides with the material.
Unornamented objects are silent, they say nothing, they
aren't praise pieces; and nevertheless the ornamented ones
don't necessarily say anything either. They have a global
function, let's say, are points of the general stage set, with
a known libretto that makes up part of the convention.

(Now an exception to this principle of Baroni's occurs to
me, which as will be seen is probably relative. It has to do
with the carving of a six- or seven-year-old boy, though
owing to his appearance he seems more like a youth. One
should think it was a branch or, rather, a modified root.
He's seated on a low chair, he has his arms open wide and
bent toward the floor, a consequence of the two branches
that issue symmetrically from the main piece of wood,
which amounts to the figure's torso. Lower down, the
trunk suddenly gets thinner and the result is a chest too
swollen for an astonishingly narrow waist. At the waist the
ribs can be made out, and the wood arches at a right angle
to become a more or less knotty branch, with gnarls and
new knots to the side, so that the boy appears to have two
shriveled legs, or one on top of the other. Thanks to the
whimsical form of this root, the doll achieves a cartoon-
like dynamism, as if he were a contortionist capable of
controlling different masses of his body. This produces
an effect of movement and of play, of mischief and felicity

that is very characteristic of Baroni. The boy is wearing a painted yellow t-shirt and on his chest an inscription says in black letters: '*Viva el Conac.*' Conac is the equivalent of the Ministry of Culture, which for decades had been helping artists by means of subsidies, commissions, support, etc. In this figure the ornamental intention has been diverted, but it's hinted at; it is definitely a t-shirt with a message. The piece expresses a vote of gratitude or of confidence, or is a nod, to an institution that has served, I suppose, as a mainstay for Baroni. And so here, too, one finds the surface to be available: the boy's smooth torso and the opportunity to fill it.)

Ornamentation would amount to one of art's possible utilitarian declensions; but there are some who regard it as the ultimate aim, or at least a condition, of the artist's work. Perhaps Baroni's painstaking dedication in seeking to resolve even the smallest details of ornament and its additions comes from religious iconography; as I said before, a way of reciprocating for favors or graces received. Because when Baroni begins to carve her first commissioned pieces, her colleagues in the craft, the wood-carvers of old, in those days for the most part made religious and laical characters in equal measure, mostly *campesino* types, austere and actually without too much coloring in their apparel, though all were of a rustic, silent, and enduring beauty. In fact, by introducing enamel on her figures, Baroni showed a new way of working with color. With this paint she conferred sheen and luminosity, she created the necessity of always taking contrast into account; and, moreover, the possibilities of color combinations were now multiplied. She proposed, shall we say, the realistic exaggeration of the attributes of elegance and of sacredness. In this way, ornamentation can also be seen as an addition that uncovers a reality until then concealed in traditional wooden figures, whether it is religious exaltation or natural exuberance.

When one is in Baroni's workshop, or when through varying circumstances one has the chance to contemplate several works of hers of varying character, one can't help but associate this work with that of another Venezuelan artist, probably the greatest in all fields. Armando Reverón was a painter who turned his life into a *modus vivendi*, and that itself into a backdrop for art. The three facets fitted together into something inseparable. He built his house, manufactured his tools, etc. The objects he was not able to make he replaced with invented surrogates (goblets made of cellophane, wooden irons and sewing machines, cardboard accordions and more). His mirror, for example, is famous; it's made of small pieces of tinfoil, which had once been used to wrap candies. His house resembled a prop room, but of a domestic theater, which requires quotation marks to be understood: Reverón made 'crowns,' 'shotguns,' 'mandolins.' The quotation marks express the borderline condition of these objects; they're useless as such but at the same time are more emblematic than the real ones. Besides that, his life's actors were his own dolls, especially female ones, on many occasions also models for his paintings, with which he would create humorous or dramatic scenes in the presence of the friends or visitors he received and in the presence of his wife (also a model for his paintings and, above all, Reverón's helper and caretaker).

Despite being surrounded by nature, living only a few meters from the sea and in the midst of the dense wilderness of the central seaboard, he lived with artificial surrogates, such as the flat paper birds he stuck inside surrogate cages of wooden sticks, or the flowers or clusters of vegetables, also of paper. A mixture of decadent spirit and tropical anchorite, Reverón seems to say that ornamentation presents alibis not only in the face of beauty but also in the face of utility. There is a use of the beautiful that is a product of artifice, which should however aim to strip it of beauty and insist on the object's utilitarian, and at the same time illusory, value. Thus the quotation marks. What is real can be false and true at the same time, as in the worlds of play, or can also be temporarily abolished in favor of the world of fantasy. In time, obviously after his death, Reverón became a kind of cultural hero. An inspired Robinson Crusoe whose intuition in the face of nature proved wiser than any education he might have left unfinished.

When I visited his house everything was already very sacred because it had been turned into a museum. It was the place where Reverón withdrew to live, still very young, after breaking with the world of academic painting and his accustomed social circle. The region he moved to has a curious name, *Las quince letras*, 'The Fifteen Letters,' the reason for which I haven't discovered to this day. Reverón called his house *El castillete*, 'The Little Castle.' They said the compound had been preserved or reproduced just as it had been during the artist's lifetime. It was a model bourgeois home, but all in 'survival' mode and attuned to make-believe and play. Not wholly theatrical but, yes, completely dramatizable, since it had not been intended for any type of audience but exclusively for a world of actors. In effect, the ambivalence proposed between a home made of theater props and the mundane normality predicated on the very variety of objects resulted in a scenario of self-sufficient austerity and self-fulfilled fantasy. The rusticity of the materials and of the finishes clashed with the simplicity of the forms and the economy of resources; this conferred on the whole a great eloquence. Outside this house, the surrounding streets (the town had grown and the wilderness been eradicated long before) and also the trees and the constructed world in general seemed frustrated attempts at life with no other option than to carry on their process of deterioration. (Years after this visit, a mudslide buried a good part of that region's coast and along with it Reverón's former house, also changing the topography of the place in passing.)

Thus, the creative ambiguity of some of Baroni's objects, not to mention her penchant for decorating every surface she had available, reminded me of the painter Reverón, who established an evasive relationship with voids, seeking to fill them even if only to set up others. The two also share the propensity toward lending their face. I already mentioned the Virgins and angels with Baroni's face. For his part, Reverón appears in the faces of the models and of his dolls, and even in the paper or canvas masks he constructed. There are paintings where a girl in the second or third plane looks out at us with an intensity that rescues her from the company of the two or three girls who accompany her; it is the face of Reverón, inserted into the disturbing nakedness of the whole. It's likely that the associations end here, since the two are scarcely comparable on any other level. The artisanal bent, obviously, the playful tendency, etc.

There are several photos of Baroni in which she is seen dressed up as an animal. They're outfits she made herself, with which she sometimes does public presentations. I've seen her in photos with her iguana and rabbit suits; and also another in which she dressed up as a poinsettia. All of them have been taken during her curious performances; Baroni moves, jumps or acts like whatever it is she's representing. In two of the photos she's surrounded by her natural space, as is true of so many others in which she's not in costume, that is, the garden of diverse, seemingly wild plants; one will also make out some typical Andean landscape painted on a wall, where people who look gigantic are walking across a gently sloping field, or some large stones marking off the path, of course decorated with garlands of green leaves and red flowers. Of Baroni's costumes one could say the same as of her figures; they're made with a similar care for detail; nonetheless the difference lies in the endeavor or the finish. The costumes bear the hallmark of domesticity, of the durability of clothes and of the tricks of dressmaking. One can imagine Baroni in her workshop sewing scraps of old garments to make the poinsettia outfit, or adapting old pants or overalls for the iguana and the rabbit. It's unmistakable how the outfits keep that look of 'altered clothing,' and how by means of this detail the viewer of the photographs verifies Baroni's commonplace dedication to simple objects and, in particular, her sense of artistic economy as an opportune use of scarcity.

The rabbit and iguana costumes have nothing added on; I mean, nothing that an iguana or a rabbit lacks. In them Baroni has adhered closely to the actual models. But in the poinsettia costume the approach is palpably free, and then Baroni draws on a good number of devices and accessories. It's odd that despite the quantity of tassels, fringes, pleatings, embroideries, seams, pipings, flaps, ribbons, bows and other flights of fancy, the costume has a simple and uncontestable elegance, as happens with even the most baroque of her wooden figures, the immense angels tricked out to impress the disbelievers, or to celebrate an event, or the women or Virgins who display their outfits with flowers, fruits, and other accessories as if it were a matter not only of the best offerings but also of the ultimate, the definitive, the utmost in exaltation and polish they can possibly attain. In each of those photos of costumes the surroundings seem silent, expectant. It's the propitious garden, the space Baroni has organized according to her desires. And in this privileged realm the iguana and the poinsettia perform, pirouetting. The rabbit as well, but it doesn't seem to me to be in Baroni's garden, but going up a wooded rise (this photo probably belongs to a previous house, the one in Isnotú or the one in Boconó). In the

three photos, Baroni looks toward the camera, caught
embodying a supposedly typical movement of the animal,
and in the middle of a harlequin's pirouette in the case of
the poinsettia. There are other outfits I haven't managed
to get a good look at, like the Bird of a Thousand Colors
or the Damsel, except perhaps in some damaged film,
where in any case what impressed me before any costume
in particular were the movements of Baroni seeking to
imitate the character in a natural way, but also turning
the scene into a species of indeterminate performance,
in which the audience was doubting the character's true
intentions, whether to inspire terror or joy, especially
owing also to the suggestive impact of her masks; at least
it's what I seemed to see in the people's faces.

Reverón also fashioned his own materials for painting,
and as visitors' stories recount, the brushes for example
were of the crudest quality, he made them with the wood
of local trees, bristles and plant fibers, and the more
worn-out they were the better they served him, because
he used them to scrape the surface of the canvas or to
distress it outright before laying on color, for which he
generally used other things. On one occasion I was able
to see some of those materials and was struck by their
coarse and seemingly urgent construction, as if they were
a set of primitive, or outright savage, weapons, whose
crudeness proved them apt for attack as well as for work.
It is very unusual to find an account of Reverón's hidden
life that doesn't express surprise, at least bewilderment
or wonder. Everyone succumbed before his virtuosity
and eccentricity, the two apparently united; indeed
there were cases of entire families who went to visit
him at his house, and even the children were surprised
at his personality and his living conditions. Well-to-do
families no doubt went because it was in Macuto, in those
days a weekend retreat, with opulent estates and resort
hotels. And since they were already there, I presume,

they devoted an afternoon to visiting the half-crazy painter, who for his part, with his trained monkey – an able artist's assistant – his other animals and his world of props, offered a complete performance of his work habits and of his preliminary rituals, or made his dolls perform, or himself assumed different roles.

It isn't hard for me to imagine the impressed gaze and the admiring attitude of the visitors in the presence of Reverón's performances; though in some cases perhaps with a feeling of condescension. It was with the animals and the children that Reverón established a more forthright and longer-lasting communication, and of a greater emotional intensity. His contact with painter colleagues grew more attenuated as his isolation on the seacoast went on, but with time, curiously, he was a point of attraction for writers, above all poets, and photographers as well. Reverón's world was a revealable element, because he himself, without realizing it, officiated as revealer. No detail in that universe proved irrelevant. Everything was contrast and outrage.

Of the roles Baroni has played, the performance of her own death has been the most notable, and, as far as I know, most frequent. In all probability I'll refer to her funerary sessions later on. In fact, as for that wooden lad with the inscription *Viva el Conac* painted on his chest, I've seen him by the side of Baroni's coffin, in one of the performances of her own death that are usually called *La mortuoria*, as if he were a boy waiting for the ritual to end, a few steps in front of an austere woman guardian in blue apparel and with her hands joined at chest height, a large, life-size carving, at first glance placed there to stand for, one supposes, vigil and consolation. This figure also bears the name of *La mortuoria*, and replaces Baroni in the coffin when she's away.

I looked once again at the photos of the costumes some time after visiting Baroni at her house; when I did it was as if I'd recaptured an important part of that land which served as a garden, until that moment forgotten or unfamiliar to me. And afterward, when I go back to look at them every so often, I pause over the whole, or over one detail in particular, and it is as if that space were updated thanks to an invisible tie, not solely the information, not even the memory, which as time passes becomes more and more incomplete, or skewed, as proves not hard to imagine, but instead the space in the most abstract and intangible sense of the word, the pulsing of the surroundings, the sense of harmony, calamity or threat, the tone of the atmosphere, I don't know. In the end, I suppose we've become accustomed to fragmentary perceptions, that's why I shouldn't be astonished by some photos that, beyond Baroni's interest or that of the person who took them, seek to refute those perceptions or posit themselves as their complement once absence has been established and forgetfulness produced.

Among Reverón's most curious objects are the paper masks. I say curious because they exemplify, in their lack of complexity, this artist's manual skills, which he conceived, I think, as the carrying out of the simplest operations so as to achieve the greatest possible eloquence. Several of them are made of brown paper. Brown paper is a material that is crude and noble in a paradoxical way, certainly far from delicate. If the real world of paintings, the actual world of life and even the imaginary world of Reverón's illusions were to have an ideal substance with which to stage a correlative, it would most likely be brown paper. Reverón made the masks by shaping the paper, making perforations and attaching a few items, like a colored dot or pieces of tinted paper, a fake bun and a false collar, or a deformed crown; but above all his way of modifying the paper was by damaging it. These faces first reflect manual labor, whose end product amounts to the representation, in its turn, of the physical destruction of the individual. Indeed, as I noted, many of those paper faces are self-portraits. I suppose they were called masks from the outset owing to pure convention, whereas it's clear that he set out to make faces, just as with his dolls he wasn't looking solely to make dolls, but wanted to construct women, subjects that were half-phantasm or automaton with whom he could exchange fantasies.

Perhaps I will mention later on, speaking in all modesty, my greatest discovery, the revelatory capacity of brown paper. In a way, those masks share the aura of mystery with many of his objects, which Reverón brought into the world as a simple tribute to their material existence, I mean, the actual objects, for lack of a better word: a real and useful existence. Whoever leafs through some catalogue of his work will be able to see not only solid wooden bottles but also piano pedals, of course apocryphal, the previously mentioned tinfoil mirror, Bibles made of sheets of newspaper, etc. The world of fantasy doesn't require complicated surrogates. And you could assume that, for Reverón, the surrogate becomes art if the material and the work are immediately reversible to their origins. An object not on the point of liquidation or exhaustion, but of reintegration into its natural state.

For instance, one thing the photos fail to show, but that I recapture each time I see them, is the incredible quantity of fallen mangoes on the grounds of Baroni's house when I visited her. There were two or three trees at the very least, you could see the half-rotten and half-buried mangoes, and also the bones, as they call the pits or seeds in Venezuela, strewn all over and no doubt lodged in

that sea of earth since the previous season. On walking
through the large front garden, you felt intoxicated by
the strong aroma of rotting mangoes. It was of course
a well-known scent, the places in Venezuela where you
don't find these trees are relatively few. Still, I had never
encountered such a high concentration. Perhaps in the
remote corner of some park, or on a lightly traveled
mountain path, you would at times begin to detect the
sweetened, slightly alcoholic fragrance, a non-animal
putrefaction, and alerted to this presence you would seek
out the sources of the aroma, later to find the squashed
mangoes scattered over the damp ground.

By means of those feeble signs, feeble since they
depended on the presence of a breeze, on the
temperature, or on the time of day, you'd at first be
bewildered, and then moments later able to establish, let's
say, a chain; to investigate the source, assign a causality
and infer the steps by which the mangoes had arrived
at this stage of advanced decay; at last you'd spot them,
they were down there, one probably under your own foot,
yellow lumps that were revealing their whitish heart,
or hearts already liberated, to varying degrees, from
their casing, some with a crown of filaments and others
picked nearly clean. Nonetheless I'd never before had the
experience of being surrounded by that pure smell; it was
like being immersed in an exclusive atmosphere, though
with no visible boundaries. I'm not exaggerating when
I say that that section of the property was studded with
mango bones; or more, that the hardest part was finding a
space free of them. To one side you could see a small brick
structure, with a tin roof, that could by no means shelter
a person. It was probably the dog's house, I don't know, it
doesn't seem so to me; or a place for housing something,
like an electric meter or a water pump, etc. In the other
area where the mangoes ended was a large birdhouse
with several parrots and macaws inside it, which were

definitely quiet the whole time, no doubt crushed by the heat and the density of the atmosphere. The recurrent song of the cicadas and its stridency added of course to the aura of suspended time, I don't know how it can be better described, of passing through an indefinite interval of that so-called eternity and which one supposes will never end. And that lethargy permeated all of it.

The rest of the plants appeared to have succumbed to the violence of the mangoes, their leaves drooping and their flowers dulled, the foliage and the silhouettes of the trees took on a somber, threatening tone despite the strong daylight; and even Baroni's little dog, whose name I don't recall, behaved as if he had lost his mind, trying to sleep on his feet while resting his flank against a large painted stone, not deigning to throw himself to the ground. On seeing such signs I became uneasy imagining the consequences that this exclusive atmosphere, as I said, could have in me; still more because the things so arranged were shaping up to be a literary or theatrical parody, those moments that can't be read and yet are read, although the scene wasn't like that at all, which itself, without a doubt, was an effect of the situation. I should say that in spite of his apparently insoluble problem, Baroni's dog, on nodding off and falling over, and on waking with a start and getting up at once, was the only individual that displayed a visible activity and in this way he helped, I think, to rescue these moments from the large-scale collapse, the general self-oblivion and the total standstill. But for reasons I'm unaware of, the animal had succumbed to the inertia and kept doing the same thing over and over again, which though it did arouse a bit of compassion and have something of a comedy routine, in any event imposed upon the scene a hallmark of desolation, of suffering and innate wretchedness. In all likelihood the dog, because of his diminutive size, was seriously intoxicated by the

mangoes. As I said, the macaws were standing around
as if they didn't exist, completely spaced-out, and the
afternoon threatened to go on endlessly without actions
or changes, abandoned to the dictates of some mysterious
local or outside entity.

But it always happens, and at a certain point the torpor
broke up as if the whole garden had completely awakened
at the same moment; I believe it coincided with the
appearance of Baroni. The oppressive fragrance turned
into the air's perfume, the trees and plants regained their
habitual splendor and even the dog felt the beneficent
effects of the change as he gave up on sleep and headed
over to his mistress. As he did I recalled scenes observed
so often in Caracas, men underneath mango trees
who would maneuver long wooden poles or hurl fallen
mangoes upward so as to knock down others; the ones
throwing were generally students from nearby schools, or
could also be the needy, and the ones who had the poles
were from the neighborhood. The prodigal tree denied
itself to no one. It was actually not unheard-of to walk
along the street and get hit by a ripe mango, something
that happened to cars as well, and they would often be
dented if the mango fell from a considerable height.

Baroni's dog was small, nearly white, restless and silent.
I regret not remembering his name, because I think it
would be somewhat revealing. At first I was tempted
to call Baroni to ask her about it, but I hesitated for a
long time and then lost interest in finding out. When
we went walking through the vast garden and while
Baroni stopped to explain the details of a plant, of a
new path, the future expansion to create a new thematic
space – something that would claim several months or
an entire year of her time – while she stood motionless
in the hot sun and explained these things in great detail,
the little dog took advantage of the pause to disappear

into the nearest thicket, surely in search of something, or investigating the novelties of the place. He would be gone for varying amounts of time, but what struck me from the first was that it was the dog, and nobody else, who seemed to dictate the tempo of the stops, because as soon as he returned, Baroni would wind up her explanation or commentary and we would set off again. It occurred once, twice, and instantly it happened again. And it ended up seeming to me, too, that Baroni's pauses obeyed those of her pet, which always preceded hers, since he generally walked a few steps ahead of his mistress, as if blazing a trail (or it could have been that the dog was already familiar with the places where she would pause). In this way, we were a group with independent but coinciding digressions. Perhaps because of the dangers he faced in that almost wild terrain, the dog had opted to penetrate the depths of the garden only when he could count on company; it was understandable, given his size. On the other hand, the garden was where Baroni spent almost all her time, with her chores and plans for topographical innovations.

From one of the passable quarters of the property you could see in the distance a high plateau. In front of it you could make out some elevated hills, at whose foot you could barely discern broad and slightly flattened valleys, dotted with fairly sporadic rounded hillocks. As I may already have mentioned, in Trujillo state it's rare to see the rugged landscape of high mountain ranges, as in the Andes. You see another kind of ruggedness. In fact, what impresses because of its captivating beauty, let's say, is the simultaneity of rock formations and abrupt folds – one might call them disorderly or even crazed – that blocked up and crashed into one another at the moment of their elevation, I suppose, along with the constant tempering of the relief, the result, on the one hand, of the time gone by since those movements, and of

the green covering that wraps nearly the whole territory,
itself a product of the hot, wet climate of the lowland
and midland areas. The gentle, endlessly overlapping
forms, which vary in steepness, direction, and projection,
producing an effect of perpetually moving planes,
nevertheless do not produce a dramatic effect, nor do
they have monumental bearing; rather, they're scenic
contours, theatrical I'd say, since the depth of any place
you look out at will never become excessively vast. And
when it ought to be vast, because of the morphology of
some formation or some terrain in particular, the clouds
and the misty areas are there to neutralize any possible
abyssal perspective. Accordingly you see diverse shades
of green, ranging from yellow-green to black-green, and
a rather wide spectrum of white, from the most absolute
brightness to the darkest gray, both colors, green and
white, with different gradations of density.

Just as we arrived at that end of the garden, I stopped
beside Baroni to listen as she explained her projects
for the near future. The flowering path will continue
through here, a rock garden, arches with climbing
vines, the garden of smiles, etc., she began telling me,
near voicelessly. The little dog took advantage of the
moment to venture into the densest thicket of all, the
least explored and the largest. We watched him disappear
into the bushes and were left there, looking straight
ahead. You could see, as I said, a plateau kilometers away,
one of those formations at times called *mesas*, which
seemed the flat platform of a mountain that rose behind
it. There were slender clouds in the shape of strands or
filaments that encircled the plateau several dozen meters
down, thinning out or breaking up, you couldn't say,
which at any rate melded with its verdant slope. From
behind, the sun lit up the plain opposite the plateau,
the plain dappled in turn with its own combination of
greens and whites, which produced a quite singular

contrasting effect because it seemed controlled, as if we were present as the stage lights came on, with their fine-tuning of climate and intensity. We stayed for a long time contemplating the view. I cannot say that this shared contemplation brought about some kind of fellow feeling, but at one moment when the light dimmed slightly I perceived the sunset, though that was still several hours away, and this made me think of the daily repeated sunsets, and it seemed to me it would be difficult to find a natural beauty that would make up for that repetition, in truth a kind of sentence. As you see, somber thoughts were knocking at my door. The garden kept producing the afternoon's habitual sounds, etc. The little dog very soon emerged from the thicket and with hardly a pause passed Baroni and took to the path again; she followed right behind him (and I along with her).

We continued our walk, were already at the midpoint of the circuit and we began to make our way back on the other side. It was curious that what couldn't now be seen, because of our new location, was there nonetheless. I'm referring to the wide-open view of the mountains, but also to the swarming greenery of the surrounding wilderness. I say curious but it's one more word; in reality it's what happens with surroundings, at once present and invisible, when they're transformed into atmosphere. That part of the garden proved fairly similar to the earlier one, the only ostensible difference lying in the wilder state of plants and botanical combinations, as if it were a matter of an advanced condition, the future moment toward which the entire place, as Baroni's personal enterprise, was pointed: the day when it would look most like the local natural world, whose closest convergence with the model, however, would be the basic premise of artifice. Some corners looked entirely well-tended, others just the opposite; not abandoned but ancient. According to what Baroni told me, it was the oldest section. Thus it made sense that the shrubbery and bushes had on the whole pervaded one another and their surroundings more, to the point of initiating a struggle in which Baroni hoped to intercede as little as possible. Logically, this area colonized some time back aroused less interest in Baroni's dog. He hardly sniffed around, and the few signs that at times seemed to excite him came from the other part, the one we'd left behind, toward which he directed his watchfulness again and again.

Baroni's conversation turned exclusively on the garden, a subject I couldn't follow as I should have because of my lack of knowledge, perhaps my lack of interest as well, but also because, as I said before, I was hardly in a position to understand what she was saying. Most difficult were the details, the names of plants or her horticultural routines, technical decisions, natural priorities, etc. But far from setting forth a description of minutiae, of a specialized nature, Baroni sought to transmit her expressive enthusiasm: she wanted a realm organized around general principles, in such a way that the result would be a more or less controlled verdant hierarchy; those principles could mask a metaphorical intention, like that same path of smiles, or they could be thematic in a horticultural sense: for instance, one single type of plant in one section, that sort of thing. Unquestionably, the garden was a sentimental and playful externalization as well. Perhaps infected by the little dog's mood, I too lost a bit of curiosity. The dog and I, unexpectedly united by a thought. And yet again, I found myself once more in a situation of the sort that happens to me repeatedly, relating to different universes of things, the moment when an initially slight uninterest announces the impending occupation of my senses and I realize it's no longer possible to do anything to save myself, until I end up succumbing to confusion, in reality a disintegration of my sensibility. The more or less recurrent bushes, the flowers alike but in different colors and the decorated stones that marked off, at times unnecessarily, the edge of the path, as I said they plunged me into a kind of torpor. I don't know if the temperature, at that moment at its high for the day, had an influence as well; whatever the case, I felt immobilized and abstracted, suspended in time, incapable of reacting, hardly able to reason. I kept forging ahead at Baroni's side, I could move, I understood whatever words happened to reach me, but I felt that I'd remained stuck a few meters back, when this sensation of absence or of emptiness, I don't know what to call it, had revealed itself. And furthermore, the thought occurred to me that despite my semblance of normal life or abnormal life, like that of any other person, I had at no moment ceased to be this way, in a state of silent stupor, immobilized by circumstances and not knowing how to behave or to think, and moreover without caring too much about it; I conceived of it as part of nature, I thought that everyone shoulders his own insensitivity or sorrow which shackles him to the floor, etc. I was incapable of blaming Baroni for my state, I knew that neither that house nor that region bore any responsibility. Besides, it was clear that if the mangoes hadn't been able to affect me before, even less could that wild garden do so now. My thing came from some other place, it was ancient and deep, or superficial and recent, who knows. I saw now that the times before when it had revealed itself I hadn't perceived it with this intensity; and afterward it had stopped revealing itself simply because my entire person was already subject to its control, and I found myself sunk in the most complete indifference. The cell of indifference everyone is born with, much like the cell of identity that each person has, in my case had grown by one of the possible methods, that is, turning itself against me.

That's how we were, walking slowly through the garden. I knew the visit was about to end, or rather that sooner

or later at some moment of that afternoon it was going
to end, and it was the same to me whether it happened
that instant or in the subsequent hours. It was my
will in submission to its own insensitivity, lulled to
sleep especially by Baroni's inscrutable words. At one
point it occurred to me to think that she was in reality
crying out for help, and that the cause of that weakened
voice lay in the practically infinite time she had gone
unheard since she'd begun her outcry. As they say, years
of bitterness and incomprehension. Much like those
crushed beings who only need someone to save them,
but most likely find no one, so that their time and their
voice begin running out. According to this conceit, I was
one of Baroni's last chances, by now there was hardly
anyone left for her to meet because she lived secluded,
in one of those dwellings hidden away in the ravines,
invisible from the highway, along which very few people
traveled in any case. The effort to articulate some
audible sentence was beyond her capabilities, exposing
her to a definitive prostration, to a life condemned to
pass with neither rescue nor salvation. I thus beheld
stupefied how she stood on tiptoe to speak to me, and
how she craned her neck in an extraordinary fashion
to draw closer to my ear, and that wasn't any use either.
I felt to blame for being so deaf and for being unable
to help. I had, however, my own problems in tow, the
numbness I mentioned was proof of them, and so I
couldn't be sure if my difficulty in understanding was
due to her condition or to my state, when nevertheless
it turned out to be clear that no great mystery existed:
what she was demanding went well beyond whatever her
words might say, that's why my comprehension didn't
necessarily pass through them.

In other words, we were facing a problem. I recalled the
rescue in which Baroni had played a leading role, when
she saved a man drowning in the waters of the ravine,

as I will certainly explain later on. She hadn't asked herself too many questions in the face of the danger, she'd decided to act on the orders of her nature, or her practical conscience or whatever. And in contrast, I was thinking of the signals and the steps to take according to some protocols that were much too slow and especially useless. It's true that her experience had been a dream; nevertheless, it was shaped as if it had been a real dilemma. That was our great difference, and perhaps the ultimate reason I couldn't help her. For Baroni there wasn't always a true distance between reality and fantasy; and I devoted my time, every day, to distinguishing what was true from what was false, with the additional problem of always keeping myself on the side of the unresolved. Nothing had sufficient weight to be truthful; even what was crudest and most material, most definitive, presented itself as provisional, or at any rate circumstantial, or, more complicated still, feeble and formless: it could happen that reality was irreconcilable with fantasy, but even so, one would end up bowing to the succession, and along with it, to oblivion, which is a form of illusion. What's the use of the truth if it doesn't endure? This was a question that, given how I felt at that moment, I could apply to all that was known, both general and personal, both what was right at hand and what was least nearby. I was finding the truth to be not only feeble, but also malleable, abject and fragile: at this point it translated as fantasy. One portion of the details of any given thing ceased to be certain, or was redundant or insufficient, and instantly the equivalent, the translation, was produced, and with it the truth was watered down.

And so we walked the final stretch of the path without saying a thing. The dog ambled on a few meters ahead introspectively, or at any rate fatigued, as if he were returning from a grueling adventure, or maybe he guessed my thoughts and even he felt ashamed of them. Every so often he turned his head, and I saw that instead of seeking out Baroni's eyes he was looking at me, no doubt wishing to verify something. We were approaching a bend, where the path turned into a verdant passageway. We were going fairly slowly, and so the shady tunnel awaiting us presented itself as a ready-made high point, something like a crowning glory. And indeed, once we had rounded the bend Baroni's house appeared, seen from behind. We were at the end of the road; and the two of us also must have seemed to be returning from a long march. I don't know why, at the sight of the house my bad thoughts were somewhat watered down; I stopped thinking of myself, if only momentarily, as an irredeemable person and I fashioned for myself an illusion of normal life, if it can be called that, surely a life hard to define. To one side of the property, behind the house, were piled some stones, junk and tools. The aroma of the mangoes returned, and now and then you could hear through a window the voice of Rogelio, who seemed to be talking on the telephone. This, too, had some effect on my change of mood; I was pleased to think that I, too, was under the influence of the house, understood as a workshop of illusions, of beings created out of will and spirit, and that the general process of bestowing life to which that place was subject included me, I was a temporary cog in that gearbox.

Not much more time went by. A while after that final look at the junk and the tools for digging in the dirt, I was emerging from Baroni's house with the confused sensation of having left something unfinished. Rogelio and Baroni stood beside each other beneath a tree, observing my departure, and they both raised a hand at the same moment, in a final goodbye before I lost sight of them. The tree was the one on which Rogelio had been painted, the one that held his mask; thus believing that they were two, they appeared, however, as three. At that moment I was unaware of having been touched by the woman on the cross; but her presence and simplicity had reached me, and I now think that my sad or disheartened mood when I said goodbye to Baroni was already a sign of her impact. As I explained above, a few hours afterward, in Boconó, the memory of the woman would keep me from sleeping, and in general everything I did on the following morning I would experience as an epiphenomenon of having contemplated her and of acquainting myself, let's say, with her existence. So then, since my spirits were somewhat depressed, on leaving Baroni's house I decided to take the longer route and delve a bit into the region of the mountain ranges. The habitual options of a crossroads, instead of going to the right I turned left. Within minutes Betijoque had nearly evaporated and I found myself, once again, before a broad panorama of mountainsides, basins, and intertwining chains of mountains. And after crossing to the highest areas of the foothills over a period of time I can't manage to recall, I took the highway detour toward Jajó, also situated atop a plateau and at a considerable altitude.

A minuscule white town, Jajó lies hidden in the heights. At that moment it looked empty, so much so that it wouldn't have disconcerted me to know, for example, that for some mysterious reason it had just been evacuated. One had scarcely a hint of anyone's presence in the houses, and along its narrow and steep cobbled streets one saw no recent signs of human activity, either. I'm a bit embarrassed because someone may think I do it on purpose, but I must say that once again I found myself confronting a habitual, all too frequent, situation: wandering like an essentially aimless stray through silent, unpeopled towns, whose meaning is as hidden as the sense of my perseverance. At the town's highest summit I found the Plaza Bolívar, obligatory, and the Cathedral; both empty. (In Venezuela the main plazas always bear Bolívar's name, with the exception of a minuscule spot lost in the depths of the country. Every village, town or city has its Plaza Bolívar, and the attributes of the Liberator's statue are also foreseeable, depending on the status of the place.) I took a seat at one end of the plaza, on a slate-colored bench near some formal gardens crossed by paths of the same color. A short time went by, from the depths surrounding the town came murmurings of wind, or perhaps they were merely, as they say, the songs of the siren of the heights. Until at a certain point I was about to end up stunned by the immovable quiet of the place. I felt that my thoughts were being wiped out and a mild drowsiness was transporting me to another place. Then I stood up and confronted the local walk.

In Jajó, as in other Andean towns, you feel immediately moved by the balance of the proportions. I guess there must be some rule of the minimum when faced with the material limit on expanding and making improvements in nearly inaccessible places. Thus, the height of the houses and the width of the streets, for example, combined with the exclusive white coloring of the walls, alongside the surrounding physical monumentality, present the picture of a human scale adapted to the natural setting, with no desire to impose itself. Unlike other places, nothing here gave me an impression of imbalance or of neglect; on the contrary, even the most incidental details seemed to respond to a simple logic and to a day-to-day organization that is, let's say, straightforward. Owing to the altitude, things in general took on a special clarity, which, considering the predominant emptiness and the bright colors of windows, doors and roofs contrasting with the white façades, gave the whole of the town a touch of measured elegance, or at least of composure, in no way dissonant with the great backdrop of peaks and high plains, with their even colors and uniform desolation. And as tends to happen, the moment arrived when so much harmony brought on an inescapable feeling of discomfiture, also of distrust.

I toured a radius of two or three blocks in the vicinity of the plaza; after the second corner the uniformity dissolved: in certain parts you could see neglect, or some façades were not in agreement with the general norm. But what struck me more was learning Jajó's limited boundaries, because when I went two or three streets farther along, I could see a plowed field, not too large, barely more than a vegetable patch, from which all the immensity of the region prevailed. There not only did the town end in the sense of houses clustered and organized, but the plateau ended as well, for on the field's far edge began the quite steep drop of one side of the mountain. You then began to descend and you found cultivated terraces, but you couldn't take that into account when it came to considering the town. Permanence and fleetingness; it seemed to me that both ideas were combined in this place alternating their habitual roles; there was no apparent contrast or conflict, what was constructed bowed to the physical command of the territory.

I returned to the Plaza Bolívar by means of a roundabout of streets. And at various corners it occurred to me to observe practically the same thing, that the actual space, the visual amplitude and the almost zenith-like, shall we say, perspective practically began a few meters from there, without the presence of transitions or mediations as are habitual on the outskirts, underscoring the straightforwardness or the candor of what was constructed. I emerged into the plaza at a different point from the one I'd entered by. The world remained as silent as before. It turns out not to be easy for me to describe the strange amalgam of silence that inhabits this town; Baroni herself when talking about Jajó stresses the silence that reigned when she happened to live there, and which obviously persists. So I emerged into the plaza, and from this angle my curiosity was aroused

by a bakery situated on the sidewalk opposite, to the right
of the Cathedral, with its exterior walls white and painted
in quite large blue letters, the name: *Virgen del Talquito.*
I didn't know that it referred to the local Virgin. I was
moved by the diminutive *-ito,* of a straightforwardness
I considered surprising, otherwise similar to that of the
town, accentuated in some way by a material, talc, that
I imagined implausible in a Virgin. (It seemed to me that
a Virgin of talc would be overly threatened, even more so
if it were a matter of a little talc.)

I've kept a photo of the bakery, taken from a few meters off,
where the name that takes up almost the entire width of
the façade is readable. The door is open, but as a result of
the brightness of the day and the dimness of the premises,
the interior is darkened and it's impossible to make out
anything. All the same, I have the memory that effectively
compensates for the darkness; when I paused to look, a
man leaned over the counter and craned his head toward
the street, trying to see me. I distinguish his face peering
out and just recognizable as if he were in the photo every
time I see it, but in reality he doesn't appear. It's also as
if the photo were speaking, because whenever I see it I
remember clearly when the man said, surely responding to
a question somebody asked him, 'He's looking,' doubtless
referring to me. His face displayed some very partial
reflections of the outside light, especially in his eyes,
just enough to notice, like those subdued ensembles of
Japanese interiors, organized around progressively indirect
and ever weaker after-effects of light.

Later on, when I was back home and the interval in Jajó
was another digressive point on my journey through the
region, associated with the other places under different
categories of things (photos, as I said, some paper with
notes, an object or a simple souvenir), I learned that the
Virgin of Talquito became the patroness of that town in

1936, when around Christmastime she appeared in some
fine sheets of talc to a young girl who was working over
them while making a Nativity. Very rarely have religious
motifs interested me; therefore I don't know whether
this apparition represented a common episode within
the panorama of the other apparitions of Virgins. I do
imagine that she did it in a time and in a way compatible
enough with the condition of the place; that it was an
obliging apparition and resulted in an evident but discreet
presence, without sensationalism; as they say, she hit upon
the right means for the town. I imagine the townspeople,
all of them half-related and gathered around the crèche,
celebrating an apparition so chancy it could have failed
at any moment, just with a higher than normal wind.
The talc-sheet girl was at that moment wearing a yellow-
flowered apron, she was a guest, she had arrived from
another town, but surely she also had some kinship with
the hosts, who I presume were involved in commerce or
the transport of goods. When the apparition of the Virgin
took place, Baroni was a little over a year old and it would
probably be just a few years until she lived in Jajó, where
she remained until she was married, at age eighteen.

After my walk, while I was sitting in the plaza nobody
went into or out of the bakery. Nor did I see people in
the adjoining streets. And yet saying the whole place was
deserted wouldn't be exactly right, because you sensed
life carrying on according to its own normality. It was
getting to be time to leave, my sleepiness came on once
again, so that I was just about to resume my journey.
Right at that moment, as I was getting up, I heard the
noise of a motor that seemed to be slowly approaching,
downshifting because of the climb. Outside of its script
lacking in action, finally Jajó was offering me something
new. Life on the periphery thrives on sporadic journeys;
that was probably the only one of the day or the afternoon.
A school bus promptly made its appearance and slowly

came to a stop by the edge of the plaza. I was already
feeling very knowledgeable about the place, but not until
the noise stopped did I notice the cloud of silence that
surrounded the town; only at times broken, at that point
in the afternoon, by the wind that, depending on its force
and direction, was bringing the murmuring of a ravine,
as it seemed to me. The driver got off the bus, took a few
steps and when he saw me was first surprised and then
raised a hand to greet me. I returned his greeting, as was
only to be expected; and as I did so I noticed that he
had no passengers. The man would have been about fifty
meters from where I was watching, he had on a white shirt
that shone too brightly in the sun. For a brief moment
he seemed bewildered, it occurred to me because of my
presence, but in the end he raised his eyes to the sky,
performed a few stretching contortions and afterward
went back to the bus to sit in the stepwell, where there was
shade. Richly deserved rest, I thought. I believed I barely
caught some music, as if he were listening to the radio,
but this turned out to be something I never could verify.
And even if at the time it wasn't an interesting enigma,
I occasionally surprise myself remembering that line
of music, as now, and would like to know if it came of a
mistaken impression or if he in fact had the radio on.

It was curious that I felt like the sole inhabitant and virtual
owner of that place, being a stranger who within the next
half hour would leave Jajó, probably forever after having
been there a brief span, equivalent to a blink, or less than
that, considering a normal lifetime. I'm not saying I felt
like an actual owner, but something resembling a mental
boss, abstract. I was looking all around and everything
came forward as a landscape that was available and ready
to be occupied at will. I was thinking, this lofty and
hidden town, so adamant at the summit, by now physically
integrated into the mountains, is nonetheless as yielding
and malleable as the most insecure particle of reality.

For a moment I feared I'd been infected by Baroni's spirit, when she invents versions of things or real events as a way of dialoguing with them, also of shaping them so they can serve as consolation, lesson or inspiration. Because while I lacked that pedagogical intention, as I believe even now I lack it, the straightforward link that she established with her objects and models of reference inspired in me a kind of attraction. It seemed to me that that innocence is a genetic code of art, and that if I wanted to speak of Baroni I ought to obey it, just as also if I wanted to speak of anything else. And I could say more: at one point I felt a strange nostalgia, or a sense of deprivation, before her capacity to establish those simple, unambiguous relationships between material objects and products of the imagination.

In this way I could define the contradictory attraction that I felt toward the figure of Baroni: I suggested a suspension of my capacities, a certain promise of happiness or instantaneous communion, but too ephemeral. I couldn't trust in the binary world of suffering or happiness, and as such I freed myself from belonging to it, which in turn compelled me to frequent it as a visitor, because in its arbitrariness and its opposite extremes I found a lost substance, in any case never attained, that operated as a promise of well-being. I mean, in Baroni's art there was, there is, a note of exaltation whose objective is betterment, in the sense of giving comfort, in life. In this respect also it coincides with religious concerns, though at times it may refer to figures that are, let's say, laical. Thus, she represented for me the infancy of art. Not only in the sense of innocence, or rather excluding that sense, but childhood as eloquence, on the one hand, as vitality, but especially as provider of life: life as contagion. In Baroni's work, one doesn't encounter the objectives of an art on the wane. There is no search for disillusionment or for irony, neither are there outright uncertainties about meaning. One puts on one's own disillusionment, shall we say, when encountering Baroni's works about herself: Baroni as object and model, resource and material.

That afternoon at Baroni's house, then, we had agreed that she would make me a saintly doctor. We settled on the price, on the time it would take to produce, it's true somewhat vague, and on the general characteristics of the piece, especially the height. After this I'd had no news from her besides a quick report on her ailing health and the damage done to her lungs by the paints. In the same way, when some months had now gone by, on the terrace in Hoyo de la Puerta I could scarcely get any more out of her about this piece. One single thing she told me, which filled me with doubts and which I took as a bad sign: she could already tell she'd have no room to put the parrot, the perennial companion of her figures, on the doctor's feet or on his shoulders. The parrot is a good omen and also, according to what they say, protects against bad luck. We were, as I said, sitting on the terrace, the sloth had already vanished into the heights of the yagrumo tree, as I will surely recount further on. Baroni must have immediately sensed my disappointment, for she went on to explain that if she didn't find a place, as she feared, she would in any case manage to put one on. (I now recall another parrot, which in the spacious garden of a house and some meters from the town cemetery, intoned the Venezuelan anthem early in the morning; hearing it, I thought that if some mourner were to visit a grave at that unusual hour, he too would hear the opening lines. But of course, in a tiny town that cemetery's morning music would be for everyone.)

As I said, I unwrapped the woman on the cross with Baroni's help and before Olga's eyes; I seemed to be receiving a present, and in truth my feeling approached that, I believed that I was being entrusted with a good, a gift or an incentive; also a kind of talisman. I grew worried about the amount of paper and plastic bags that covered the piece. The bags belonged to businesses in different cities; stores in Valera, Boconó, Maracay and Caracas were represented, also Barquisimeto. One could trace a line between these places and imagine a tour in episodes, with departures and arrivals, partial detours and setbacks. I should say that at that moment these bags moved me as much as the wooden woman on the cross herself; they were her seasoning of daily life, of life pure and simple, the proof of Baroni's little private and domestic world, certainly made up of commissions, local journeys, visits to friends or family, workshops, hustle and bustle, artistic invitations, etc. And from each of those trips, I thought, a bag would also remain, or more than one, as proof or unsought souvenir. Not only their utility, but also the good sense in keeping them was verified in cases like these of the woman on the cross. And it was another proof of the immediacy of her presence. On the round stone table the constituent parts of the delivery were separated then: the woman, the sheets of newspaper, and the bags from the stores. Papers and bags seemed the tools the woman on the cross would make use of for her relocations, and also for a moment I thought that her elegant boots and attractive dancing dress, and even the piping that adorned her neck and her shoulders, which had clearly been added to elevate her attire, I thought that all of that had been bought in those places and that the bags had come all the way here as proof of authenticity. An existential proof, shall we say, because Baroni had dressed the woman with these pieces obtained in those stores, and a productive proof, the most valuable of all, concerning as it does a made figure, because it demonstrated that Baroni had used that same clothing to realize the work.

I was tempted then to save these bags as proofs, and
didn't hesitate to make up my mind accordingly days
later. They would be the frame, the complement of
reality, the cultural documentation, I don't know;
and also, I thought, they would be the Venezuelan
foundation. The connection of life and geography that,
while it seemed tangible because of its superficiality, in
reality almost always escaped me, I have no idea why, or
at any rate I tended habitually to put it in an unreachable
place, verifiable only in the presence of a certain type
of signal, like the bags or situations like this one I'm
describing, in some way chancy in their result. The
bags told a story incidental, aslant or complementary
to Baroni's own; and they also showed a history lateral
to the one of my approach, or access, to the woman on
the cross. Sometime later, when I said goodbye, I would
take the bags with me with the excuse of protecting the
figure, which however I hadn't imagined surrounded by
this plastic altar, wrinkled and deformed at first sight.
A mundane and sacrificial heroine, the woman on the
cross insisted on offerings of paper and plastic. In reality,
the stage set of bags from the more or less traditional
shops of Valera, Maracay, or even Barinas accompanied
the woman on the cross to a few meters from here,
where I am now, until not long ago. It was like a territory
circumscribed by the figure's demands, where perpetual
but frozen disorder reigned, since nothing moved in that
space above which the woman stood upright, absorbed,
as always, dominating all of it from her severe height.
The bags seemed strewn about at random, as if she had
shoved them carelessly aside in her haste to get dressed
and clamber up onto the simple pedestal from which she
has never come down.

At the house in Hoyo de la Puerta they invited me to
some fruit juice. We talked a bit about the weather and
another bit about the people of the place. In Venezuela,

to talk about the weather means to talk about rain or the lack of it. Around that time of year, the leading observation was that every year it rained more than the previous one; the dry season grew shorter and a larger area was getting inundated and was subject to flooding or mudslides. The other topic turned out to be more unexpected; Olga said that, for some time, a good number of the people she saw in the area were unfamiliar to her. At times she crossed paths with acquaintances of hers who were talking with strangers, something that aroused her curiosity still more. And among all the strangers, the most worrisome were the children, because logically she connected them to her acquaintances. There were no teenagers. I asked her if she by now had acquaintances who until a short time before belonged to the group of people she didn't know. She said yes, but that in due course they'd become part of the group of the new people, not of the strangers. That is, there had been relays, surges of new people. A while back I had read items in the newspapers about the peopling of the area (they had used the word 'sudden'); they also said it had been messy. Now I'm thinking it over, and it's astonishing how much you need newspapers to know a country, or at least to believe you know it. Given the topography of the place, the changes weren't easy to see. You could be on a street or on the highway and see various people coming from the ravine or some low-lying area, from their houses or shanty towns, to wait for transportation.

And once again I felt the backward leap, the strange sensation of recurrence, the repetition of a familiar experience, in this case a news item that I was seeing confirmed as if it had been written to be compared with one's own experience. Every so often Baroni would break into Olga's story with some diminutive or expression of affection, or of outright compassion.

In those parts, at the time less urban than now, unfamiliar people engendered wariness before curiosity.
Nonetheless, Baroni's friend was herself unfamiliar to
the new people who'd arrived with their families, close
friends or neighbors from another location.

Olga was explaining this – difficult to explain as she
acknowledged – when Baroni, who had since some
moments before withdrawn from the conversation,
stretched out her arm and without saying a thing pointed
ahead of her: up the trunk of a nearby tree, which rose
out of the verdant depths, a sloth was climbing. We
sat in silence before the apparition. Not because it was
known did one fail to be overcome by its slowness; and
that happened to the three of us, as if the animal were
teaching us a new style of movement or, still more, as if
it were acting for us and were proposing a suspension
of time. Once again we ascertained that it's not easy to
keep your eyes on a sloth for an extended time span,
because the slowness engraved a kind of weariness on
its movements and this made the event seem of little
importance. That's why you would turn your eyes some
place else, or would simply get distracted, and later
when you'd look again the animal would still be in the
same place, or at least that's what it would seem like,
as if the intermission hadn't occurred. We went on
keeping an eye on it in this way, adrift, inserting at
intervals disparate comments about any old thing.
Something unexpected was about to happen, though:
the sloth was several meters above us, it seemed focused
on its ascent, when it decided to turn its head and stare
at us. As if we were one single reaction, the three of us
sat astonished at such a human behavior: turning to look,
I mean, displaying something that resembled curiosity.
We saw its face, similar to a clown's; or its entire body
resembling a doll. At that moment we could expect that
it would stay immobile for a long time, because each

change in position represented a span of eternity, and
yet before we knew it the animal had already undertaken
its normal ascent. At times it turned its neck a hundred
and eighty degrees and leaned out backward to look
down; and it did it so efficiently that it seemed we were
witnessing a form of contortionism, once again human.

(I will now allow myself an informational parenthesis,
like those old movies that take a little detour so as to
show aspects of local life. The slowness of these animals,
appropriate enough when they're moving through the
trees, turns into a dangerous awkwardness when they
happen to walk on the ground, where they're exposed
to deadly hazards. On the outskirts of Caracas it's not
uncommon to see sloths flattened on the pavement
or lifeless on the shoulder of the road. At the same
time, anybody who wants to assist one, for example,
in crossing the highway and so tries to carry it, runs
the risk that the animal will grip him with those claws
suitable for climbing very tall tree trunks, in an embrace
that's difficult to undo and capable of sinking to the
bone. Because of this, and because of logging, it was
normal to see fewer and fewer sloths.)

The animal then resumed the ascent, in the face of
which our conversation would always seem minor, a
superfluous concern and an extravagant use of time.
Nonetheless minutes later it repeated the operation of
looking down. I recalled then that on another occasion
I was watching, as now, the movement of a sloth when
rain and heavy winds let loose. It wasn't an overly intense
rain, yet the gusts were enough that in a few minutes the
animal was soaked, and motionless and clutching the
yagrumo with all its might, it displayed, shall we say, the
true shape of its angular body, like a small and emaciated
cat. That tree, which generally serves as protection from
the rain, and so affords the sloth shelter besides food,

didn't have enough leaves. I could see then that this
animal's volume is composed almost exclusively of fur;
that its true body, if it's possible to say it that way, seemed
at least in this case subject to a regimen of exhaustion
and that its skull was the size of a mandarin orange,
moreover not too large.

With the passage of time, the stage set of bags around
the woman on the cross was gradually turning into a
ravaged landscape; the plastic aged, took on a shadowy
patina, lost color and pliancy. The figure of the woman
on the cross looked exalted as the days went on, and the
bags, on the contrary, changed character to become a
sad and shabby presence. One morning it seemed to me
that with their combination of grime and murkiness they
were absorbing the energy or nature of the woman, itself
probably very limited (they were her audience and stage
set, I thought, and as such they were consuming her),
consequently I decided to remove them; they had now
more than fulfilled their testimonial role, the woman was
capable of carrying on alone with her pensive expression,
with no need of any crèche or diorama.

There came a moment in which we forgot about the
sloth; it must have continued its slow-moving ascent.
We said something about that territory, about other
countries, among them my own, about the people from
each one of them, etc., and it was obvious how during
this entire conversation Baroni always tended to speak
of herself and about three basic topics, which could be
summed up in the words health, feelings and creation.
When I had met her at her house, this inclination
seemed natural and worthy of attention, not to mention
given her weakened state and the fact of its being a first
meeting; now however it seemed a habitual limitation.
'Artists are like that, always in their own world,' Olga
told me at a moment when Baroni went out to talk on the

phone, wanting perhaps to justify her, to understand her, or maybe seeking to establish some complicity; according to her way of seeing things, I think, she and I: two people belonging to the world of practical things. It was obviously a mistaken vision, though I didn't say so. Nobody could argue that Baroni didn't belong to the same world as Olga, or to the same world as I. On the contrary, she's generally someone very attentive to crucial aspects of her activity, which she seldom neglects. On one occasion, she protested to the organizers of a juried creative-arts show because her work had been included under the heading 'popular art.' Baroni demanded a spot in the general art space, without preset categories. The organizers did not accept her protest, though in any case she got it on the record. It was when she delivered the saintly doctor to me, about a year after the meeting in Hoyo de la Puerta.

Baroni had to travel to Maracay, where the creative arts biennial took place, to receive the prize in the same 'popular art' category. There she would state her protest, even when she didn't yet know if she would accept the prize (she ended up accepting it). We agreed by phone that she would take the saint to Maracay for me, where I would go to pick it up. Maracay is some hundred kilometers from Caracas, to the occident, as they say in Venezuela. It's a hot city, one of the various and long-term dictators who governed the country, Juan Vicente Gómez, had resided there. As one enters Maracay, from any point, one sees enormous military installations that seem never to end. Once again, I met up with Baroni at the house of a woman friend of hers. Because of various details it seemed like a scene copied from Hoyo de la Puerta: the house on the outskirts, the area of Taca-Taca, neighboring Maracay, the garden or patio, which in this case looked out onto an especially dense thicket, from whose indistinguishable depths came the sound

of a stream or waterfall, the stone table in the middle of
a patio where the saintly doctor was waiting, etc. This
time, Baroni hadn't wrapped him in plastic bags. He
was protected with blankets or simple scraps of fabric,
surely remnants of old clothing. I'm not exaggerating if
I say that when we took off his vestments and uncovered
him, the saintly doctor for a few moments disrupted the
equilibrium around him, that is, us and the surrounding
natural setting. I knew from Baroni that the doctor was
going to be holding up a child; she had also warned me of
the difficulties with the parrot.

I should say that I felt immediately confused, and it
should serve as explanation enough. My confusion
originated in the complete presence that can be attained
only by beauty, maybe that's not the right word, let's
say handsomeness, more neutral, a luminescence, who
knows, the aesthetic emphasis. The greens of the foliage
became still more nuanced, and the few objects present
(the table, already mentioned, some wooden seats and
two rocking chairs) seemed to find a more trustworthy
meaning than their foreseeable practical use, which was,
once again, to serve as a frame for the visiting doctor.
Baroni's figures count on that capacity, to subject the
surroundings to their presence. For its part, the work
exhibited in the Salon of the biennial was a quite tall
Virgin of the Mirror, of nearly life-size proportions and
super-baroque. It belonged to the group of works that
were adorned with varied colors and small wooden pieces
or additions, which amounted to lacework, pleatings or
borders on the clothing, bodily ornaments, etc.

From what I could find out, the Virgin of the Mirror has
occupied since Colonial times a fairly minor place among
the Virgins at the disposal of the faithful in Venezuela.
She appeared in Mérida, a bucolic city in the Andes,
reflected in a small and inexpensive hand mirror, of the

kind known as a dime-a-dozen. Nonetheless, perhaps conforming to her needy condition, she was the Virgin who restored Baroni's sight after three dreams that put an end to two years of blindness, probably brought on by nerves. Once her vision was restored, Baroni made her first carving, dedicated to the Virgin of the Mirror in gratitude. A figure twenty-five centimeters high that she placed on a wooden block by way of a pedestal and kept on view, as she says, in order to show her to everyone who comes to her house. In reality, the recovery of her sight was a more gradual process, with two apparitions of the Virgin. In the first dream, Baroni finds herself crying and there appears to her a long-haired girl, about nine years old, who asks her what's wrong. Baroni answers that her eyes are spoiled, and that's why she's crying. The girl then promises to heal her. When Baroni wants to know who she is, the girl responds that she's the Virgin of the Mirror. That is, it was the sign. The second dream has more reversals. In it Baroni goes to bathe in a ravine of Mesa de Esnujaque, the town where she was born; it's the Ravine of the Virgin. There she sees a man who is drowning and there's nobody in sight who can help him. So she dives into the water and lifts him onto her shoulders to bring him to safety.

We can imagine the bewilderment of the man, to whom it must have seemed unheard-of that a feeble woman, moreover blind, would be able to lift him. A moment later Baroni senses that her face is bathed in blood. Still carrying the man she immerses herself so as to rinse her eyes, and little by little she notices that the pain is going away and her eyes, sunken until that moment because of the blindness, move forward, recover their former pressure and return to their place. She rinses her face several times and by now when she touches them they don't hurt her; a moment later she has recovered her sight. With these two dreams Baroni started seeing again. As an expression of gratitude, she gets a small tree trunk and carves the figure of the Virgin, as I said, of some twenty-five centimeters, which she decides to keep on view in her house. To that end she places her on a log of considerable size. Nonetheless, the Virgin will appear in another dream, the third time, to ask her a favor: she requires a greater presence and so Baroni must make her larger. She tells her to use the log that she, the Virgin, rests on. It was the second step in the dissemination of the Virgin of the Mirror in Baroni's charge. Later on, this large image will be the one that heads religious processions in Boconó.

Bracelets, ribbons, jewelry, crowns, flowers, the colorful additions of Baroni's Virgins, which fill the figures and their garments, come to compensate for the simple schema of bodily representation, but they also confirm or underscore the straightforwardness of that same frontality, which is, shall we say, sculptural, perhaps a bit antiquated, but of palpable eloquence. Though the Virgins may wear a great quantity of accessories and ornaments, they keep on being simple, modest and discreet. Religiousness lies in their expression, on various occasions called hieratic; humility, for its part, comes from the bodily posture, leaning forward; and the abundant adornments amount to a display of the spirituality, the nuances, of Baroni's personal devotion.

Meanwhile, the miracles begin as soon as Baroni finishes the first Virgin, of twenty-five centimeters. The first one has as its protagonist a gamecock, when they place it at her feet, mortally wounded. It spends the night beside the Virgin and the following morning the animal has recovered, hungry but ready to brave the experiences of any gamecock. This new miracle was the beginning of a renewed era for the Virgin of the Mirror, who found in Baroni an intermediary who was virtuosic in several senses of the word. As we all know, a mortally wounded gamecock is generally an animal doomed by its physical condition, though it can keep a claim on our attention. No one writes off the fighting cock that seems defeated, because everyone thinks that they're capable of getting over their own pain. It's even possible for the defeated cock to attract new wagers; it is the case in the so-called 'Bolívar' bet, which puts odds of five to one on the apparently defeated bird. The fight hasn't ended but it seems decisive; but every so often a cock draws strength from who knows where, sets upon the other, supposedly victorious one, and finishes it off. On one occasion I wanted to organize my ideas and asked Barreto, a friend, about these 'Bolívar' bets. I had a somewhat baroque memory of the mechanism: I thought you were betting on the amount of time the seemingly defeated cock would keep alive the fighting instinct of the other cock, the winner. It was a nonsensical and unworkable idea. From my limited visits to the cockpits and from my conversations with Barreto I could gather, among other things, that cockfighting is one of those hidden brotherhoods that transcends borders, and, if it could, any other human boundary. It's likely that further on I will explain some complex facets of my friend Barreto.

I'm not familiar with the motivations of this miracle, if it was coincidence or if there was a specific reason for a gamecock to be the protagonist of the first episode of healing, if some linkage existed with Baroni's then recent healing, etc. I never asked her; I'd like to have known, even if it were a matter of the more accidental course of events, but I didn't do so and now I regret it. In general I regret having asked her so few things, perhaps I was too inhibited before her slightly secluded and self-sufficient world that led her, as I said, to speak almost always of herself, whether of dreams, pains, joys or ideas for the future. For only a brief time could one establish a relationship between Baroni and the mortally wounded bird. The one coinciding point would be the struggle for life and the obvious proximity of death. But the usual attributes of a gamecock, the instinct for supremacy and especially its formidable aggressiveness, are as far as I know absent, and it's not hard to guess that it's actually so, in Baroni. There is probably an arbitrary relationship; in the end, the same reality often establishes and conceals the linkages in a pretty surprising way. The mortally wounded cock manages to survive, nonetheless being a victim of its own nature, which leads it to die or to kill and outside of that probably finds no object, let's say, for its existence. Consequently, its attachment to life, if such a thing is verifiable, signifies its desire to fight once more. But there is always a previous moment that cockfighting devotees, and of course also the cocks, seem to know very well; it's when the cock receives the different wound, the decisive one that dooms it and puts it out of play, after which it falls back and stays still, sometimes tired and at others with no evident interest in survival. It can happen in any case that a cock will get up and fight once more. Everyone at the fight will get to their feet, frenzied and loudly cheering the animal on, or reviling it; anyway. In those cases, people might say that the wounded cock regained its strength, though this ends up being evident for the briefest of times. It's that the cock, even though nearly dead and barely able to draw breath, the only thing it wants is to kill.

The compassion of the Virgin of the Mirror, embodied in this first figure of Baroni's, addressed itself then toward a being with those characteristics, ruthless and innocent at once, perhaps commiserating, the Virgin, over the weakness and suffering of the victim. During her period of blindness, Baroni learned to knit by hand, an art in which she achieved unusual skill, the occasion for praise from those who knew her around then. It was when she was hospitalized for her mental condition. She asked to knit and they didn't give her needles; the director of the place declared she could only have yarn. Another of the things I failed to ask her was whether after her cure she kept on knitting; although I imagine not, that knitting was temporary work and a little autistic, shall we say, to carry her through the darkness and the psychological collapse. In any case I've seen a reportage they made of her where Baroni knits for a few moments. I took notice of course of the astonishing agility of her fingers, but what impressed me more was seeing the expression of her lost stare, in whose emptiness her eyes seemed to recover their blindness.

After the second piece, Baroni kept on making Virgins of the Mirror. Also new figures and different religious scenes where, from the outset, she tended to combine elements of doctrine, popular beliefs or lore, local customs, nature, etc. Ever since her first vicissitudes in Boconó, when she lived in the cemetery, or later, when after some studies she devoted herself to taking care of the sick and to 'fixing up the dead,' as she says, Baroni's name, or her image, achieved local fame with relative ease. By the time she was eleven, with the first cataleptic attack she became known for having special powers. The people from the surrounding area wanted the holy young woman to cure their illnesses or simply to see what the rest didn't know; the future, for example, or malaise in its broadest sense. Baroni recounts that in the solitude of the town, in this case Escuque, where she spent part of her early childhood and later years, at night she generally covered herself with whatever was at hand and began to ululate, as it was supposed the spirits did. During her childhood her mother taught her to carve wood, a calling she abandoned until the miracle of the Virgin.

With the carvings of the Virgin of the Mirror there occurred something similar to her fame as a healer and seer. At the start she obtained a local fame of enthusiastic comments, which went on spreading outward and whose result translated into commissions. Practically ever since then Baroni hasn't stopped making her figures, and as their correlative she tackled a series of artistic initiatives, or cultural ones in general, addressed to her objects of veneration on the one hand, that is, the Virgin and death, and on the other to the local community, of neighbors and nearby towns. In the city of Isnotú, where she lived for several years, she made a museum in her house, logically called Museum of the Mirror. It was the place she devoted to exhibiting her work, nonreligious work also, and to praising the Virgin. Even today, leaving Isnotú in the direction of Betijoque, you find on the right-hand side of the highway the former Museum of the Mirror, where a son of Baroni's now lives, Marco Tulio by name, also a woodcarver. Once I stopped at that house – as imposing as a castle, at whose foot there's a fairly large parking lot, as if it were a tourist spot – and after I'd rung the bell for a while a skinny little boy appeared. He told me the house was closed and that it would open some days later, though he didn't know when. I've seen a film where the son carries Baroni in his arms. He's a heavyset man and you see that lifting his mother takes him no effort at all, for him it must have been like pushing a chisel along a piece of wood. And Baroni is to be seen with her insecure expression, which is how she always appears on camera, very apprehensive of the interviewer's reaction. I don't know the reasons for Baroni's move from Isnotú to Betijoque, or the reasons for the previous moves either, for instance when she left Boconó, where she had a house she was building with Rogelio, the property of which, according to what Baroni says, had no end in the back, it reached all the way to a stream and she dreamed of extending it. There,

in Boconó, they had a small grocery at the front of the
house, where they sold canned goods and perishables.

Isnotú is situated where the heights begin after Valera,
in the midst of a mountainous landscape, of course,
and on the road to the cordillera. It is the town where
the saintly doctor was born, and today practically the
entire place is turned into a shrine of veneration; at any
rate all the visible town, because the part not devoted to
the Venerable, as they call him in keeping with his title
on the road to sainthood, has turned invisible to any
visitor. Whole blocks dedicated to the sale of religious
trinkets, and on the opposite sidewalk facilities
prepared for worship per se: chapels, monuments,
altars, convents, prayer walls and offering walls, etc. In
Isnotú one can see in concentrated form the efforts of
the Church and of local merchants to regulate a fairly
irregular devotion. Spirituality fades away and yields
space to the creation and satisfaction of religious needs.
Thus, the saintly doctor assumes all portable formats,
and when veneration needs to remain manifest in the
shrine, whether as gratitude, debt, or favor beseeched,
it gets translated into a metallic plaque surrounded
by thousands of others, generally pretty similar, that
populate the walls of an almost monumental enclosure.
I stood for a while in front of the densest wall and I
didn't really know what to think, because each plaque
seemed to fade away among the rest, and they all made
up a curious, anonymous piece of writing.

I don't know if there's an official prohibition against
the painted or homemade ex-votos, always singular
in their expressiveness, but if it doesn't exist, the
impediment currently in force seems in any case
to be absolutely effective. Unlike other popular
devotions, as far as I know the saintly doctor's is not
used to transmit teachings or lessons from his life.

By coincidence I arrived in Isnotú two days after the
doctor's birthday. Since he was born right there, his
birth is also commemorated. In the rest of the country
he is celebrated on the day of his death. Signs of the
festivity's end could still be seen; despite which the
townspeople seemed instantaneously adapted to the
small-town normality, receiving occasional visitors like
us on weekdays, as if the habit of the celebrations were
just that: an assemblage of the worshippers every so
often, on weekends, or for two or three days over the
course of the year, and then the return to the normal life
of a shrine on call.

Opposite the house of offerings, to give it some name,
in the bakery I went into to have a coffee to recover from
the time spent crossing downtown Valera – a feverish
assemblage of vans, cars, street vendors and pedestrians
amid a steamy heat – in that bakery I could observe
vestiges of the heavier-than-normal business during
the saint's birthday: a good quantity of dishware on
the tables, piles of accoutrements not about to be used,
but recently yes, stacked boxes of empty containers,
disposable plastic bags, etc. And as counterpoint to
these signs of activity, at a certain moment, probably
hectic, were the two or three regular customers, almost
invisible and to whom no one was paying attention.
And especially there was the atmosphere, which
conveyed a climate not of constant mediocrity but of
practical neglect, a kind of life without its own life, I
don't know, like those small-town bus terminals that
outside of movement and foreseen events remain sunken
in shadow and indifference. From the counter, the
shrine and the whole main street of Isnotú made up an
over-the-top scenario, of well-consummated indulgence.
In the offerings building the color black predominated;
they were the metallic plaques that shone in the daylight
like a perturbing mausoleum, which seemed erected

to instill fear. If you went closer you made out other colors: plaques of sky blue and red. As you read them you witnessed a nearly always identical text on them all, which had a formula for gratitude, generally the words 'thank you,' the initials and surname of the person, or the entire family, the date, etc.

At that house on the outskirts of Maracay we sat then contemplating the saintly doctor for a good long time. There wasn't much conversation outside of our remarking, each in turn and with exclamations or scattered phrases, on the way in which the doctor was imposing his presence on that backdrop of plants and on ourselves. At a certain moment we listened to the siren of an ambulance. A few hundred meters away was the highway that connected Maracay to the sea; a road that goes over the mountain and through the majestic rain forest that covers it. Baroni sat in thought: her eyes turned toward the ground in a gesture that I was somehow familiar with because of the woman on the cross. A moment afterward, retrieved from her absence of mind, it seems to me, by the siren of another ambulance we heard passing, she told me she'd had to buy a bus ticket for the doctor, because otherwise they wouldn't have allowed her to put him beside her, on the adjacent seat. And having dismissed sending him as baggage for fear he'd be damaged, she couldn't have held him on her lap the entire night, either, on account of the weight. So that the doctor had to have his ticket, as she related. In this way, some eighty-five years after his selfless death, the saintly doctor repeated the voyage he must have made so often during his lifetime, from Trujillo to Caracas, although of course under other circumstances and by different roads. Now he was making a layover in Maracay, where he would change companions. For that, I'd brought with me, in the same backpack I used in Hoyo de la Puerta, the small and

simultaneously large quantity of necessary bills. We
therefore repeated the operation, I took out the payment
and handed it over to Baroni. I obviously had to pay
for the saint's ticket, and once again I had some mixed
feelings regarding this purchase, let's say, which in this
case extended also to the trip.

The money seemed insufficient, incapable of representing
what I was appropriating for myself, but at the same time
it was the right magnitude for attesting to the change
of hands. I felt I was not only buying the piece that
now stands, cracked and split, as I've said, a few meters
from here, but that I was also appropriating his recent
nighttime journey in a traveler's place, was buying that
type of related, and somehow so symbolic, vicissitude;
but above all, I trusted that I was appropriating the time
and the effort (the inclination and the attitude) that
Baroni had put into the making of the figure. I'm not
saying that the saintly doctor was secondary; on the
contrary, he was the center of the question. But through
him, now being mine, I was saying: a minimal part of the
scant strength Baroni still conserves, a bit of her immense
or unknown talent, even a fraction of her physical
deterioration, the consequence of working with her arms
and especially of her contact with the paints, I bought all
of that and it belongs to me in an ambiguous way, yes, or
rather a diffuse way, and yet completely true. Accordingly,
ever since then what stays with me is the idea of being the
owner of immaterial things, but as if they were material;
and in particular, something that hadn't happened to
me with the purchase of the woman on the cross, I felt
that through these operations I was borrowing part of
Baroni's life, that I wasn't only buying a moderately
mute and fairly eloquent object – that could definitely be
controversial – but that I was also assigning myself part
of what that object had had as its motivation. And so,
I thought while Baroni counted the money onto her

lap and went on leaving small piles of bills on the table, a fairly infinite chain could perhaps ensue. My appropriation reached all the way to the saintly doctor, or still further, toward some incidents from his mysterious life and in particular his imposing legend.

The sun was filtering through the garden's wet branches and unevenly illuminated the wooden body of the doctor. He shone like a recently finished piece, logically, and at his feet the dark scraps, parts of old pieces of cloth or worn-out blankets, represented the vestiges of his long journey, I'm not referring to that recent one taken beside Baroni, but proof of his far-flung and choppy journey, as much civil as religious and immaterial, in the form of worship. In this garden and on this table he found rest after a long time, etc. Everything could adapt itself to a more or less idyllic version of the saint; I did not care to force or manipulate anyone's story or intentions, I wanted to take it as the real version, as the manifestation, let's say, of that yieldingness of life I referred to above. In this sense, my illusion simply obeyed Baroni's instructions. They weren't defined, or even explicit instructions; I could sum this up by saying that they were her attempts to produce a history, a context and a theatrical space for her works. Hence the true or imaginary episodes with which she surrounded the figures and her work on each of them (of adornment, of scenographic commentary, but also of theatrical digression). Anyhow, the fact is that that ensemble of scraps and wool around the saintly doctor on the stone table seemed to me an essential part of him; as it stood, the ensemble was another of Baroni's combined pieces, something like installations, or inanimate performances. As I said much earlier, she had made of her life, in its different depths and lines of continuity, a work of art, obviously fairly scattered, and also uniform and multifaceted at once. And in that sense one could always

discover 'something more' on call, a real complement or
some element proceeding from the situation's context or
from the weight of the past. In Baroni the impress of the
artistic was open, and as a result everything, many things,
could join in and change each element.

I'm not sure what thoughts the doctor might have today
about his birthplace, even considering that they've set him
up as a hero and he serves as their breadwinner. When
he happened to work here, shortly after his graduation,
he complained about the inhabitants; in his letters he
expressed outrage that they still believed in 'el daño,'
the damage, that is, in evil spirits, spells or superstitions
in general, chickens and black cows. The feeling was
reciprocal; being native to the place and having family in
the town did not make him more estimable to the people,
on the contrary, many hated him or at least scorned
him. Those letters are from 1888. Almost every day he
made the journey to Betijoque to tend the sick and to
see if he'd received any mail from Caracas or any new
scientific journals. He was eager to leave Isnotú, a place
he wound up loathing, so that he tried his luck in Valera,
Boconó and even in Andean villages where he must have
alighted sidestepping the ice. But each place already had
its doctors, or its resistance. At one point they began
grumbling about him as a 'godo,' Goth, so he decided to
write some of his letters using Gothic script, to which
end he always carried a calligraphy manual; he feared
they would banish him to Caracas or, worse, send him
to jail. Thus he justified the use of the German alphabet,
as he called it, so that they wouldn't be able to read his
letters. Nevertheless there might have been other reasons;
for example, romantic relationships whose character he
needed to keep hidden.

As had happened with the woman on the cross, the saintly
doctor was also accompanied for quite some time by

his former wrapping. The pieces of cloth and remnants, all dark colored, provided a slightly gloomy setting that was, however, quite authentic, because immediately one thought of episodes and parables of a biblical, prophetic or sacrificial type, and of a pastoral type, in its bucolic or wild version. For example, there's a famous photo of the doctor riding his mule, on what seems to be a mountain path near Isnotú, surely taken on one of his daily trips to Betijoque. In that photo he's dressed with his habitual modern elegance. More than one person, when contemplating the figure of the saintly doctor in my home, believed that those clothes had belonged to him, or in any case that he could have worn them, and that they now rested at his feet as proof of his selfless evolution, on the one hand, or as documents in themselves, I mean, similar to sudaries, proofs of his labors. Many of those who thought that way were not familiar with the great man nor did they imagine his abiding religious inspiration; nonetheless they came to perceive it thanks to the arrangement of the whole. In truth, up to now I've referred several times to the people who exhibit some reaction, generally vigorous and enthusiastic, even in some cases, as is apparent, of a stupefying credulity, in the presence of the saintly doctor and the woman on the cross. I should say, however, that there is also another type of friend, to whom these two personages say almost nothing, people who pass by in front of them and leave them behind as if they were two invisible beings or at most members of a secret ritual group that cannot help but inspire distrust.

The day after my phone call to Baroni to ask about the woman on the cross and to agree on her saving it, I was leaving Boconó. It was a reasonable hour of the morning, the early and coolest moments had passed and the sun was beginning to get hot. An intercity bus passed in the opposite direction, and for a split second it seemed I had spotted somebody, peering out the window to see me,

of whom I'd had no news for a long time. I believe we
managed to make eye contact, but before there was any
confirmation, the route, as they say, had us part ways. After
that I encountered a caravan of vehicles that was moving
pretty slowly along the highway, in the same direction. The
curves didn't allow the cars in the rear to pass, besides they
were bumper to bumper and kept at such an even distance
that they seemed a kind of convoy being dragged along
from ahead. In front went a fairly battered small truck, but
the two pickups behind it and the final car looked worse,
which made you think they actually were being towed. I
guessed that the pickups and the truck were for farm work,
or something related; now they were carrying families, five
or six people apiece. Some were on their feet, holding onto
the sides of the truck bed and looking off to either side,
others sat with their backs against the cab, in which case
their eyes were fixed on the cars to the rear, that is, on the
section of the road, one could say the part of the world,
that they'd just left, in a kind of constant verification.

At the police checkpoint they paused for a short while
before going on; the same later on, when they were
apparently also stopped at the military checkpoint. On
each occasion, as they set off again they took their time
reaching the regular slow speed. On the left the mountains
rose, to the right lay a broad sinuous valley, its riverbed
hidden in the depths most of the time. As is easy to
imagine, a considerable line of cars would form behind
the caravan; and as soon as some were able to pass the
line would be renewed. When I left behind the turnoff
to Valera, which goes up the mountain on a narrow and
intermittent strip of pavement, invaded on both flanks
by the surrounding greenery, I darted ahead of the rural
convoy. And later, at the height of a dirt road parallel
to the highway that goes down at a very steep drop, an
impracticable chute for many vehicles, the convoy was
already pretty much forgotten.

I don't know the name of that steeply sloping road, but if you want to go to Juan Andrade's house you must go up it. Andrade is another prizewinning woodcarver, he lives in a tiny village in the heights, whose name I failed to jot down, inhabited by families who farm. Some of the houses are old, with the solidity and size of another era; others belong to a more recent time and you can generally see that they were built with the bare minimum, or even the bare essentials, so as to remain from the outset half-built. Among the many differences between Andrade and Baroni is the fact that he's very quiet, almost mute, he speaks as little as possible. His figures can be religious or not, he can make campesinos or patriotic characters. Andrade's religious carvings are sometimes very determined by the official iconography, because people frequently request saints the same as the ones that appear on altars in churches or on prayer cards, which they bring as a pattern when they arrange the commission. According to what Andrade told me, he has no preferences for making one type of image or another, although the sacred ones, to give them a name, take him longer, and so he charges more for them. Still, I think, he must make them like a rigorous copyist, excluding the occasional dictates of creativity.

His own figures, the imaginative ones, shall we say, are pretty dark, they always seem angry, or at least on the defensive. On the afternoon I saw him he took me to his workshop, built meters away from his plain house. Two of his sons were there, working or playing with some tools. On a high shelf, in the back of the shed and close to the ceiling, I saw a standing mermaid who seemed to have been forgotten for quite some time. Despite what must have been considered disadvantageous – the accumulated dust, the by now faded colors, the murkiness owing to the passage of time, the flawed resolution of the piece and even the unfinished state

of an important part of it – this mermaid was of a beauty
so resolute that from her height she revealed herself
to be one of those divinities whom no one notices but
whose influence reaches everyone. Andrade's youngest
son had made this piece, and I can say that the mermaid
now stands on a piece of furniture, a few meters from
a large window through which you can see another
mountain and a good part of another valley which serves
as her backdrop.

A few moments ago I saw the mermaid once again in a
photo I've kept, and I remain struck by her prepubescent
air and above all the definitive authenticity of her face.
Her breasts have scarcely budded, and her body sketches
a curious arc, imitating the waning moon, or a scythe,
tipped to the left as if she didn't understand something
and had to adjust her body to see or hear better. That
tilt also recalls Baroni's Virgins, invariably canted,
especially the head, whose effort to lean to the left at
times becomes dramatic and makes one think of the
arduousness of that position, of course in case it's real. In
fact, the attitude of the Virgins is so telling that that tilt
has been interpreted as an attribute of humility. Therein
lies one of the most eloquent contrasts in many of her
religious figures, which on the one hand are ornamented
as if they were exotic princesses, and on the other have
a bodily stance that is helpless, insecure, as if their will
were about to be overcome.

Another son of Andrade's, some years older, named
Carlos Luis, had an image of Simon Bolívar. It's
common to make Bolívar, since he belongs as much to
patriotic devotion as to popular religion. This Bolívar's
uniform is turquoise and its trimmings golden; his boots
are black, as is his hair, furrowed in waves. His arms
hang fast to his body, but his hands have been resolved
in different ways, because while the left is extended

downward and follows the line of the body, the right exhibits a hollowed-out fist, barely open, which is where he should be holding his saber. When I saw the figure, the empty hand was noticeable. So I pointed out the absence to Andrade and asked him if he'd lost the saber in some battle, or if it was an excess of historical fidelity (the whereabouts of Bolívar's saber have been unknown for years). Andrade gave a chuckle, it seemed to me he preferred to ignore the joke, maybe out of shyness, I don't know, and he replied that his son wasn't there, but if I wanted he could make the saber himself that moment; 'In just a minute,' I believe he said. Then he took the first piece of wood he found on the floor and began cutting. Because of the haste, I suppose, or our eyes on him, the result was something closer to a knife, even a facón. The thing is that in under five minutes it was ready and he gave it to his youngest son so he could paint it golden, like the epaulets and other attributes of the outfit. This Bolívar is some fifty centimeters tall, and impresses one because of his features, which are pronounced, and because of his body, of portly proportions and lines. One looks him over and he seems to be suffering from a migraine or to have a special nervous sensibility, because his brow is so prominent that it recalls the standard facial features of social realism.

Now, at this moment, the turquoise Bolívar holds his knife a few meters from where I sit, and his expression of anger endures, and together with his Lombrosian skull, of course insensible, they grow ever more aloof from their distant Andean origins. Sometimes visitors who look at him are surprised at his hollowed face, which gives him an expression of watchfulness and now and then, depending on the light, of a mind feverish and apt to inspire dread, of a Romantic type, all of which makes one think of his body, whether by contrast or antithesis, a body of heroic proportions. At my behest, Andrade

months later made another saintly doctor. In those
days, I was at the height of my veneration, and each
figure I acquired implied a perfected commitment to
the saint, at any rate a more consummated one. Part of
the doctor's success is due to people's needing neither
the Church or its intermediaries in order to establish
a relationship with him; and in this sense I considered
myself fortunate, because it offered me the possibility
of persevering in a variable belief, regulated by me
alone, with its own arcs of intensity and detachment.
A soft belief, in all probability, but the only one that
allowed me to glimpse the experience of a true religion.
This religion could be too elementary, it's true, it could
even fail to be considered a religion but instead a mere
syndrome, an attitude, if one wants to infer from it
some sickly connotation, because of course it didn't
add up to a system of beliefs and spiritual norms;
nonetheless that didn't matter to me, it was my easy
religion, or rather the religious icon I had decided to
adopt. In reality not because I sincerely believed in the
doctor's healing power, or his being a bulwark against
sickness and pain in general, but because joining in the
worship was the only way of being attentive, let's say, to
his manifestations; but at the same time, owing to my
devotional deficit, those concrete expressions became
the center of my curiosity and, more, of my belief, so
that what interested me about the saintly doctor were
his ubiquity and his versatile condition, the different
forms he could assume within the habitual repertoire
of his figure and, in fact, the way in which people
looked at themselves through him.

Several months went by until one day I received
Andrade's shipment. And to my enthusiastic surprise,
the saintly doctor proved to be almost outlandish.
I was working back then in an office in downtown
Caracas, and my co-workers stood stock-still before

the figure, especially superb because of the astonishment
he provokes. He is some sixty centimeters tall. He draws
your attention not so much because of his body's strange
proportions – legs too short and a nonexistent neck –
but because he's carrying in his hand a violin. In other
representations the doctor carries a medical bag or can
wear a stethoscope hanging from his neck; I've seen
some with umbrellas, there's one who has a syringe in his
hand, there are several with books or even with a suitcase,
not to mention the one who carries the Child, made by
Baroni. There's another carving where he's represented
at the fatal moment in which he was run over; the doctor
has his arms up, half-trapped under the car. Nonetheless
I'd never happened to see a saintly doctor with violin.
As I told my co-workers – in an unintentionally priestly
tone, it seems to me – faced with these situations it's best
to keep quiet and not wonder too much. To a degree the
artist's decision is unfathomable, and any explanation
he offers us will turn out to be hard to believe, useless or
disappointing, even if it in fact illuminates the work. The
doctor with violin also stands a few meters from here,
his time of frozen life elapsing. On a certain occasion,
one of the many visitors who come to look at the pieces
asked me how it was that the doctor ever managed to play
the violin if he had no space between head and shoulder.
Sometimes practical questions are not relevant, I think,
although at the same time, taking life for granted makes
them inescapable.

The deceptive capacity to confer existence is another of
the things that attract me and at the same time frighten
me about these figures. These doctors of silent life, in
reality idle to the degree that I don't require them to
practice their calling as devotional images, which stand a
few meters off, keeping up between themselves an interior
conversation, especially because it's a matter of several
incarnations of the same personage, would doubtless not

exist to manifest themselves if I hadn't commissioned
them and, to describe the operation in material terms,
if I hadn't been willing to hand over money in exchange
for them. I'm not speaking of the serial doctors, the
plaster figures or the statuettes of different sizes generally
imported from China in the tens of thousands that in
any event are produced independently of my will, but
whose manufacture and existence, on the other hand,
also attracts me and which I'd never put an end to, even
if I had the capacity to do so. Thanks to their multiple
proliferation (from artisanal pieces to artistic stylization,
passing through serial superproduction), the individuality
of the doctor, from my point of view, is accentuated
and acquires a different consistency depending on the
circumstances. His now distant real life becomes more
abstract, but his existence, as individual experience, is
revealed as tangible, even within the illusion that he is all
this, thanks in great measure to his representation.

Andrade told me that his two daughters were living
in Caracas, where they worked; and that it was his
three sons, all younger, who were with him. Seeing the
workshop you could immediately tell that his work as
an artisan was occasional, it depended on commissions,
which since he lived far away and in the middle of
the mountains always proved sporadic. He therefore
depended above all on competitions. He would make
some piece for the occasion and given his extraordinary
talent he always won one of the top prizes; he then went
to Boconó, to Valera, rarely to Caracas, to wherever it was,
received the prize money, saved if he could the newspaper
clipping where he was praised and immediately went back
home. On the right-hand wall of his workshop, on a shelf
that runs from one end to the other, I saw before I left,
small and isolated, a plastic saintly doctor. One of those
figures from China I just mentioned, which reproduce
the doctor's best-known photograph, probably taken on

57th Street in New York at the time of a brief residence,
where he poses seriously, almost rigidly, with his hands
behind his back. Leaning against the wall, behind the
doctor, a pair of prayer cards that formed a kind of court
or altar guarded his flanks. Almost all of those doctors
from China have slanted eyes, something that seems
to conform to a terrible mistake in the factory mold.
But that doesn't make them any less in demand, since
in one respect, as proves logical, belief responds to the
form's most general contents and disregards the details.
A short time ago, opposite the church where the saintly
doctor is venerated, in Caracas, I saw at one of the stalls
of religious articles a new Chinese version of the doctor,
with the eyes not as slanted but the hat a bit different
from the usual. He was wrapped in transparent plastic,
that so-called cling wrap that's used to cover foodstuffs.
It seemed to me the most appropriate wrapping, and
that's how he remains, a few meters from where I am
now. That cling wrap, I think during my exercises
in spiritual or religious fiction, amounts to tangible
irradiation, aura revealed. The representation of a force
field that obviously exceeds the mere cling wrap, but
that is made manifest almost tangibly thanks to the
sfumato of the wrapping, which resembles a translucent
spider web.

We left the workshop and I walked with Andrade some
thirty meters. It was the highest part of the mountain,
translated into a domed plateau, with scattered trees
and divided into parcels. Farther on Andrade's youngest
son was running here and there; and the dog, which had
been dozing the whole time as if it had had a big meal,
raced around eagerly, hanging on what the boy would
do. The temperature at those heights was lower than
in Boconó by several degrees, which was borne out in
Andrade's dark, tight-fitting clothing, also in that of his
sons. As I was saying, I then left behind the steep turnoff

that goes from the highway to Andrade's house, and I'm not exaggerating when I say that at that moment the four-vehicle convoy was absent from my immediate memory. It probably kept on advancing at its slow speed, who knows; some of the passengers in the back would still be on their feet, just like the children, two or three, seeking to catch the hard, cool wind. When I had overtaken the truck in front, I'd made out somebody sleeping in the center of the truck bed, face down and head to the side, one arm as a pillow and his free hand over his eyes.

I went along the highway toward the lowlands, where the mountain ranges come to an end; obviously, to the same degree the road I was on gradually descended. I was thinking about those mountains behind me and I found it hard to understand, as now to explain it, perhaps I'll make an attempt farther along, I sensed that I was leaving a one-of-a-kind, unrepeatable place. Contrary to my many or few known places, this region had immediately endeared itself to me. Even now I don't know if it was Baroni's influence or the erased and reconstructed traces, in another register, of the saintly doctor; or if it was actually the physical condition of the land. Perhaps owing to its spectacularity, though I still hadn't completely left it behind, those places became accessible to me only as abstractions. I didn't feel I was leaving a region of defined dimensions and characteristics, a *paese*, as the Italians would say, but was above all leaving a representation, a stage set. I imagined a sketch or small-scale maquette where my actual displacement appeared. The geographic features were signaled by their names, with an indistinct point almost at the edge of the page, which turned out to be myself, moving farther away. That drawing included everything. I was aware that it was a map, and of the most arbitrary and artificial kind imaginable, which nevertheless rendered this moment of the journey more true.

A while later a fairly sharp curve appeared, where a sign on
the right indicated the turnoff to San Miguel de Boconó.
I went that way, it was a sinuous, descending road that
reached the depths of the valley, where the town and the
river lie. In San Miguel de Boconó, Colonial buildings
alternate with other, less venerable ones, belonging to
different eras. The street plan has stayed the same in
the center of town; but farther on, in the areas where,
as I said, in Jajó you found emptiness and immensity,
here there are buildings or empty lots that disrupt the
typical checkerboard, some times because of the purpose
assigned to the properties and at other times owing to the
characteristics of the area, surrounded by ravines. What
seems most historic is the church and some houses in the
blocks surrounding it. One of them was pretty much a
mess, as were many others, but I remember it because a
placard referenced the local committee of the governing
party, in those days the MVR, despite which it seemed
abandoned. In any event it was morning and, as happens
in small towns, it wasn't easy to tell if this solitude was due
to some temporary absence or a permanent one, to break-
time or to some routine of the place.

When they lay themselves out this way, as emptied places,
testimony to an improbable but feasible abandonment,
etc., whose life reveals itself by way of intervals, otherwise
unknown to us, towns like San Miguel de Boconó have
always produced a feeling of melancholy in me. But
of course, it depends on the observer; and in general,
the outsider looks at the surface. You could see several
groceries and a bakery were open. The other businesses
seemed closed, though actually you had to knock on the
door or ring the bell for them to wait on you. The plaza,
modernized at some point in recent decades, was nearly
deserted and two or three people had gathered, without
speaking, on the corner opposite the church. Owing to
the grade of the terrain the plaza has two or more levels,

and from the highest one farthest from the hollow of the
ravine, you see the church as if it were a sunken building,
or disproportionately dwarfed. This church is one of
the oldest in the region and from what they'd told me, it
preserved on its walls painted ex-votos that expressed the
devotion and gratitude of the parishioners for miracles
or favors received. I had been hoping to find what doesn't
exist in Isnotú, but as will immediately be evident this
wasn't possible either.

The church was closed. I asked the men of the plaza
about it and they told me that it ought to open because
an *angelito*, a dead child, was about to arrive, but they
didn't know when. They also pointed me to the house of
a neighbor woman who kept the key, on the next block,
so I could ask her to open it. I went there, rang the bell,
waited a while, and finally a woman came out of the
house opposite. She told me that the church was closed,
and would only open in special cases or on Sundays.
I responded that they'd told me an *angelito* would be
arriving. This aroused her attention, or curiosity, and she
wanted to know when; but obviously I didn't know how
to answer her. I went back to the church without knowing
what to do; it was curious how any visitor, for example
myself, recently disembarked and planning a casual visit,
settled into the rhythm of the place and in a few minutes
became something like an inert presence, as if one had
no shadow, incorporated into the mechanics of the place,
at the mercy of its dark or trivial forces, but at the same
time, because of one's condition, was transformed into
an unexpected accelerator of local information. Pretty
resigned that my visit was ending at that moment, I paused
on the church porch to look out at the plaza and the rest
of the town. The plaza had little vegetation. The renovation
had consisted in equalizing the natural irregularities of the
terrain according to the levels, and so steps and pathways
abounded, circumscribing the earthen flower beds. Two

of the men crossed the street to find out what the neighbor had told me; I told them she didn't know anything and that she'd told me she didn't have a key. So they pointed out a second place where I could ask for it, because if this neighbor didn't know about the *angelito*, he wasn't coming.

The other house was downhill, a few meters from the ravine. The irregular terrain made it a bit difficult to get to, and as you went down you heard the increasing noisiness of the water. There were two children playing in an open patio, behind an iron fence. Past the door, which was open, two women were cooking. One of them came out and to my question said she didn't have a key, but she advised me to go to the pharmacy, facing the plaza, on the side opposite the church. The premises of the pharmacy were apparently small, though one couldn't tell because behind both the window and the door white curtains concealed the interior. I rang the bell more than once, as indicated, and waited in vain. I asked someone who was walking by; this person told me that if I rang the bell and they didn't answer it meant that it was closed. All the people I dealt with said goodbye to me in a way that was cordial and distant, almost ceremonious. Even the neighbors across from the church, with whom I had by now spoken more than once, resumed and ended each conversation as if it were the first, and probably the last, that we were having. I returned to the church and protected myself from the sun on one side of the porch, wondering about my next step. I viewed the gentle slope of the streets and in the distance, stretches of the winding road to the Boconó highway, surrounded by greenery and thickets. The clouds, as I suppose happens daily over the course of some months, were indecisive about releasing the mountains, in a kind of symbolic embrace, so often celebrated in the descriptions of many regions of this country.

I began thinking and noticed that in this place I could feel
myself to be, so to speak, in the midst of crumpled paper.
I was in a valley, surrounded by various ravines, near a
rocky river, and with chains of overlapping mountains
in sight in the distance, and a series of knolls or rounded
hillsides closer by, of irregular heights and arranged in
an arbitrary fashion. This was how a friend had some
time before explained to me the geography of the state of
Trujillo: 'If you get hold of a fairly thick piece of paper,
crumple it and try to make a ball, and then try to flatten
it out only halfway, that's a pretty close replica of what
happened in Trujillo.' Despite colluvial fans, alluvial
streambeds, fluvial terraces, millennial erosions and in
general all of nature's actions aimed at leveling relief, the
landscape kept on displaying a majestic craziness; not
because of its heights, by now fairly notched, but because
of the visual arrangement of the ensembles, an outcome,
they say, of the continuous counterpoint of faults and
foldings. Even today there are movements in that land,
which never finishes settling, and occasionally more
than once a day. And as to the severity of the weather the
outlook has, of course, always been the same. There is no
witness or chronicler who has failed to underscore the
capricious nature of the temperature, which goes from
cold to hot, and vice versa, in the shortest of distances,
often independently of changes in altitude. That long-
ago succession of formidable geological movements
had compressed volumes in every direction, producing
that effect of disorder and disorientation. The disorder,
on the one hand, gave one a sensation of provisional
landscape, of undecided and even chancy geography, and
the disorientation was simply the wildest epiphenomenon
of the difficulties in communication and access. So I
imagined I was seeing a crumpled piece of paper, and that
there, at a confluence of wrinkles and creases, I stood
indiscernible, looking out into the distance. From that
piece of paper you were unable to leave.

In the meantime, I began hesitating as well between continuing my journey or staying a while longer, without doing much of anything, and in hopes that one of the neighbor women or someone in the pharmacy, any one of those people would commiserate and open the church for me. I was absorbed in these vacillations when a gentleman from the plaza who had just hurried across interrupted me: after the new greeting, he said, 'Here it comes.' I wanted to know what he was talking about, and with his head he gestured to the entrance to the town; 'El angelito,' he added. The procession from the highway was approaching along the main street. Now they went forward more slowly. Those who were traveling on foot had to brace each other better because of the unevenness of the paving stones; and you could also see how all of them, faced with the new scenario, surrounded by houses and intersections, paid renewed attention to what was going on. In some fashion that I can't explain even now, the woman from the other block was already opening the church before the procession came into the plaza.

Since I was a few steps away, I went in immediately. It took me a while to get used to the darkness of the church. The windows were scanty and of dark glass, so that very little light filtered through. Seen from inside, the ceiling turned out to be less high than you would expect. I went up to the famous left-hand wall, which people had told me about enthusiastically, but the miracles were no longer hanging there. I guessed I'd have no one to ask; the woman had vanished toward the back – she didn't return while I remained in the church – I believe to open some curtains, since an oblique, almost horizontal light immediately entered from behind. I went over to the door again. The caravan had stopped opposite the porch and people began to get out. Moments later they took from the back seat of the car, without any great effort and with quite some care, a small coffin, of approximately sixty centimeters.

I noticed that on the highway I would never have been
able to see that it was a funeral cortège, or in the town,
either. That occasioned in me, on the one hand, a feeling
of disappointment: once again I confirmed that it's
generally very hard to be aware of everything; and on the
other hand, I had a sensation of bitterness at attending
the drama, or rather one of its scenes, interwoven so
firmly into everyday life with not much notice. The two
points, disappointment and bitterness, were each sides of
the same fact. In the group of mourners there were older
men and women, some teenagers and various children.
The man I'd seen sleeping on the highway woke up at
this moment, when the rest were already waiting on the
porch, probably a signal. He got to his feet, took a few
steps to the back of the truck bed and stumbled, falling
onto the street. At first no one came over to help him. I
thought he was probably stunned, only later did I notice
that he was drunk. He remained lying in the street
without moving. It occurred to me to wonder if perhaps
that wouldn't be the signal; then they went to help him.
But the man began throwing punches and kicking as if
he were defending himself, while yelling things I didn't
manage to understand, clearly offensive and repressed at
the same time, to go by the impression I had. Afterward
he stood up before the eyes of the rest, made as if to
smooth his clothing, though without success, and took
a few steps that were not entirely straight.

The church had had its former importance, the central
nave was deep, but perhaps because of the prolonged
decline of the place it now seemed fairly austere. In the
corners of the side aisles were cornices with saints carved
in wood. I was looking at one of these saints, so simple
and artistic at once, when the cortège passed behind me
carrying the child's coffin. They set it down at the back
of the nave, in the dimness of the altar. The women took
their places at a certain distance, encircling it, the men

went off and stayed outside the church, and the children, for their part, near their mothers, walked around, peeked over the coffin and immediately jumped back holding their noses. Outside or inside, nobody spoke. They had dressed in their best clothes for an event that despite their travels and sudden reversals was not being resolved. According to what I learned, they had hoped to find a priest to officiate the Mass and help them bury the child. They traveled from town to town, where they were turned away because they had no death certificate. The child had gotten sick and had died, apparently without anyone's intervention. At this point I started thinking and I didn't quite know how to go on. I, who believed I reasoned in a more or less constant fashion, met an unforeseen activity interrupting the flow, while irregular, of thought. Was this, once again, a signal or some type of warning? I don't know. I imagined Baroni's reaction, since she was probably used to rural experiences of this nature, interjecting phrases of sincere compassion on learning of the news and invoking some saint or protective figure, who knows, or harking back to some similar incident from the past.

Baroni's opinion is that death is a habitual juncture in the general sense of the word, toward which we are not only irrevocably heading; one can also cross that threshold various times, let's say, and return to everyone's surprise (except hers, obviously). It is her experience, following the attacks or episodes of catalepsy she went through ever since early childhood; a fact that, viewed from the future, perhaps shaped some traits of her personality. As I said before, her fame as a healer and spiritual seer began at the time of that early experience. She herself acknowledges that she doesn't fear death, because of having lived through it, so to speak, on various occasions. The second experience, as an adult, lasted three days: the first, as I described, twenty-four hours. Baroni recounts that in both cases they wept over her inconsolably; until at a certain moment she got up, frightening her relatives out of their wits. She also thinks that we should coexist with the possibility of death, and always be prepared, as she says in her case for when the hour arrives. For that she has built in one part of the garden, alongside a mango tree, her own funerary altar which is a kind of retreat. There sits the coffin, which she made by hand, and invariably inside it lies *La mortuoria*, a carved figure, as I described earlier, an approximate replica of herself, that leaves the coffin only to yield its place to Baroni. There are also different objects that allude to or are suitable for these rituals.

From time to time Baroni performs her own funeral: she dresses in the appropriate attire, a blue dress, which she put together for that purpose, and she lies down in the coffin, homemade as well, where she remains motionless for a long time. Why is the dress blue? Because they dressed her in that color when she died the first time. As she herself says, she gets into the coffin every Good Friday; and lying there she is capable of foreseeing various important things that will happen in the next twelve months. She also stages her death on other dates or in other places, or it may also happen that, in obedience to an urgent inner need, she'll take her blue dress and go to the bier, where she'll stay for a variable period of time. Lying in the casket, Baroni finds peace and immerses herself in transcendental thoughts. Friends or occasional curiosity-seekers come over to her house to see her. Other times school groups arrive from the surrounding area, with whom after the funerary performance per se she speaks on related subjects under the mango tree, on some half-buried rocks painted with multicolored motifs that she has arranged in a circle for this type of conversation. This circular space amounts to the anteroom of the mortuary chapel.

Baroni has performed her death at other sites as well, for example museums. They're performance cycles that can last several days, and sometimes end in the cemetery, just as she's about to be buried, after the funeral procession. During these shows, when Baroni is not in the coffin *La mortuoria* takes her place. The audience members join in as the visitors at a wake; and of course, if Baroni takes a break from her role, that is, when she's not occupying the coffin, she almost always speaks with the audience and recounts her experiences. These performances, as I said before, bear the name of *La mortuoria*, the figure that serves as her replica and when it isn't replacing her represents someone undefined, a sort of coffin-guardian character, a pensive being or, rather, a pious one, also always present, otherwise, at the crèches Baroni prepares for Christmastime. So that Baroni's familiarity with death is exhibited in several recognized ways.

She therefore doesn't miss the days that elapsed in the cemetery. When she arrived in Boconó and found no work, the money she had wasn't enough even for her first night in the plainest *pensión*; so while asking she went on walking to the cemetery. That was the most suitable place to live, surely because of the confidence and security it provided her at that moment. And also the following period, devoted more professionally to the practices of nursing and especially the laying out of the dead, as well as later years, probably all of them should be deemed a proof of the intimately necrophilic life she has led since she was small. On various occasions Baroni has said that she's always healed the sick and laid out the dead. Her girlhood dream was to be a nurse when she grew up; for that she had a black doll that she always doctored and gave injections to. She knows about medicinal herbs by way of her mother, an expert on the subject. And after age eleven, as I said before, she began healing with her hands and giving solace. Dressing the dead was also something she did from early on, and especially, as she says, the preparation of the *angelitos*. Even once time had passed, when Baroni was already a prizewinning artist, as of a few years ago she still continued to lay out the dead, especially the people who'd been crippled for a long time, for which she had no problems lying down on top of them and working on them until she'd left them in an appropriate position.

When Baroni is asked about the deaths she had, she says they were two, four, or at times she declares another number. This variable quantity, I believe, doesn't conform only to some symbolic intentionality, to which otherwise any person has a right, or to some loose definition of the verb 'to die,' as when it's said that something or other that happened 'was to die for'; if it were so, it would be, though legitimate, a supremely trivial answer. It seems to me instead that it conforms to her multiple experiences relating to death: events took place of a different type, of varying degrees of profundity and of diverse resonances, for which there is always, however, one same verb, which is 'to die.' In fact, I think that reminiscences in general present this problem, though obviously to a different degree. Because, for example, the memories of different events, even of a different nature, while connected by one same owner, as might be one's self or one same consciousness, necessitates a catalog of words and phrases ample enough that they're able to stand out from all the other events and reminiscences. And if it isn't possible to draw upon that catalog two options then present themselves: the standardization that comes of silence, or action as a way of maintaining the diversity of memory. That is to say, perhaps the dramatization of death is the form in which Baroni describes or evokes her own diffuse experiences, impossible to express with all their shadings in any other way.

Although Baroni maintains that death holds no fears for her, at a certain moment I wanted to know if dying for real during a performance of *La mortuoria* would for her be the same or different; and in case it was different, how and why. Somehow, I thought, she would need to get up to put an end to her performance, to return to the world of the living with all her qualities unscathed; and if it didn't happen that way, it would turn into an unfinished performance, or a truthful performance, without any acting. In this sense, it has the menace of any theatrical performance, which is the risk of interruption. She told me that when she stretched out in the coffin after having gone over the arrangement of each of the scene's elements and her own attire in general, her intention was to honor and pay a visit to death, that the rest would happen when it had to take place. It was a preparatory exercise for herself and a lesson for the rest. This was the only thing she said to me on this point, although in other words.

I've seen several photos of *La mortuoria* and unfortunately the people in the audience have their backs turned, or their heads down, in any event, the visitors' reactions aren't visible; I imagine that those expressions are always revealing. You see in the foreground Baroni lying in the coffin and around her the semicircle of people, looking at her. I've also seen, not long ago, some footage of several funeral performances. I didn't expect to discover anything in particular, but I was struck by the theatrical emphasis in the first I saw, which was grade-schoolish, as one might say. The clearly defined roles for Baroni's helpers, the scolding priest, the pair of lovers who kiss each other in that woeful scene, the wailing women, etc., and how they played their roles according to a fairly strict arrangement. The children were off to one side, but I don't believe they were acting; and as I had seen in San Miguel de Boconó, in this case, too, they peeked out over the coffin. In this performance, let's call it museumesque, Baroni wakes while they're keeping vigil over her. She gets to her feet and begins to recite a glorification of death; they get the microphone to her moments afterward, so that the first part is lost. The audience reacts with surprise, as if it were witnessing a miracle.

The other footage doesn't take place in a museum and looks like a home movie, though it brings together more people because the whole town takes part in the staging. Therefore the actors are 'real,' they half-act, they do what is strictly directed within their natural deportment. At one moment, when everything is set to leave for the cemetery, the priest appears who says, in a scarcely ecclesiastical tone, 'Brothers and sisters, we're now going to give a Christian burial to señora Rafaela.' Then several men approach, hoist the coffin as if it were a piece of furniture and go out to the street. I also made notes of one of the final scenes. By now the funeral cortège has toured through the narrow streets. I calculate that over two hundred people followed Baroni in her coffin, in what seemed, to go by the faces of the people, a religious procession. They get to the cemetery, there are some nuns who look very sad. And when they set the box down alongside the grave, one step from burying her, Baroni wakes up, or comes back to life, sits up and embraces the person who's beside her. Standing up on the coffin, she begins to recite the poem of funereal glorification. She speaks of the 'plain chamber' where they'll be keeping vigil over her and she describes different details and steps of the ceremony.

Sometimes Baroni gets other numbers ready. She persuades people to act and assigns the roles. Farther along I will perhaps refer to the marriage ceremony, a less frequent performance. But now I'd like to reiterate my wonder at this performance, which set me down once again alongside that kind of childlikeness or straightforwardness in art that I referred to before, which undoubtedly makes it more kindred to the religious festivals and traditions of the Andean towns than to sophisticated theatrical forms. But plainly, some are able to appreciate in it the complexity of what's simple, a species of forbidden fruit for others. Truly I have taken no position on this matter, nor on almost any other, either. Farther along I'll probably refer to certain problems of representation, for lack of a better term, and a kind of curiosity, or shortage, that I feel sometimes when I see how what is dark and arduous for me is visible and negotiable for others.

There's a story of a sick person, at the final moment of his strength. He spends his days in his bedroom, lying down, and in an almost completely unconsciousness state. When he happens to wake up, he opens his eyes and looks around him; it's the only thing he does. He sweeps his eyes over everything, but devotes the same attention to the people and the things. The person taking care of him notices one day that his weakness increases when he receives a greater number of visitors. It happens at night, people have gotten out of work and can go see the sick man. Then the bedroom fills up and, the person taking care of him thinks, each visitor absorbs part of the scant energy the terminally ill man still has. It's not that among them all they divide up what there is that day, a kind of uniform ration that might impose a little rationality on the senseless advance of the illness; on the contrary, the visitors are savages, each one unconsciously claims his or her own share. For that reason a greater flow of visitors, so to speak, reduces the sick man's life.

Now I see that the descriptions of these vigils, with the semicircle of people around the bed, are fairly similar to Baroni's stagings, including the ones for school-age

audiences. In the story it's understood, if I remember
correctly, that the sightlines of the people's gazes are
the channel in which the flow of energy circulates;
not the sick man's gaze, though, whose eyes are lost
and inscrutable almost all the time, but the gazes of
the others, transformed every night into concerned
witnesses who nonetheless transcend their most explicit
volition, obviously related to their good wishes and
their hopes for a recovery. Apart from that, it would
be an error to suppose that the energy lost by the sick
man gets transferred to the visitors; my impression is
that the energy is dissipated in the flow of gazes. It's
the price of, or rather the wastage generated by the
dramatic tension. What are the visitors seeking? If one
could intercept their gazes one would discover what
they see, as living mirrors. It's what I wasn't able to do
at the vigils of *La mortuoria* I had the chance to see; in
some cases because of a disadvantageous placement,
for me, of the audience members, and in others because
of my own lack of inclination. As I've said, beneath
that mango tree Baroni has built a crypt for herself
where she every now and then lies down, occasionally
for an audience of students who are interested in
this experience, which afterward, I suppose, will get
poured into written work for the class or into group
presentations, or even into comments at home.

I'm not aware of Baroni's plans relating to her body; if
it will rest definitively in this tomb when, as she says,
her hour arrives. It must be a very special temptation
for someone who has conceived of her house as a
museum. Whatever the case, the staging of one's own
funeral rite proves dramatically sustainable if the
protagonist periodically gets up and does 'something'
as the inhabitant of the two districts; a binary creature
capable of coming and going at will, given that a too
prolonged immobility could be inopportune from

the theatrical point of view. That's why Baroni as
protagonist must walk around, talk, hold forth. Nor
can she get out of the coffin and stand aloof, in silence
and avoiding any communication, because that could
be interpreted as a continuation of the show by other
means; a metaphorization of death, not its display.
Besides, pleading fatigue after playing dead would not be
altogether credible. In this way, during the intermission
direct communication takes place with the audience,
without hierarchies; and the intermissions define
the amphibious beings, characters who come and go
between different worlds. I never asked Baroni if she had
any regular schedule for organizing these funeral scenes.
La mortuoria links together distanced worlds. Not only
life and death, but also the present and the past of the
community, the private world and the public sphere,
etc. It also creates a breach in the audience's perception,
because it offers details about something that hasn't
happened yet. Between that actual evening or night on
which they attend Baroni's staging, and the true moment
of her death, is a still undetermined time that, by means
of the performance, emerges as a negative ellipsis.

Probably those attending are scouting out, so to speak,
Baroni's eternal rest and also their own. Even faced with
the photos of *La mortuoria*, whether on the occasion
of museum performances, popular festivals or in the
domestic space of her own garden, one cannot help
but accept death itself as an inevitably social event,
in the first place, and a starkly theatrical one (beyond
the true theatricality that the occurrence in each case
is going to assume). Another aspect is that, for its
part, *La mortuoria* proposes a tangible, present-day
version of the rural district's legends (that catalogue
of beliefs which the saintly doctor condemned in his
phrase about believing in '*el daño*'), with its cast of
apparitions, magical locations, fantastic animals, etc.

Not because she tries to reproduce or modify them
(on the contrary, periodically Baroni proposes to
disseminate and preserve them), but because she
reinstates the mechanism of coming and going between
the shadows and the light, the belonging to two worlds.
The reiterated performance of a death that is inevitably
unique lays out in its theatrical confidence the same
logic on which the proliferation of carved figures
rests, and it presents, like these, an initial argument
for adoration. In this way, Baroni's death is also an
ideological fact; this allows its exhibition to consist of
the staging of the funerary rite; and its possession of a
true correlative (although it's reversed: the actual fact,
while it belongs to the future, has its own ideological
correlative) doesn't mean that Baroni's death when it
happens for real is going to refute it.

I think once again of the poet Sánchez, especially of the
funerary rite over which he happened to reign, so real
and true in his case that he probably didn't even realize
it, in the face of which Baroni's performances seem a
simple commemorative aspiration impelled by a spirit
of mimicry. Death, religion, nature. Baroni's innocent
art turns and spins on these surfaces, it seems to me,
not only because they coincide with her central artistic
preoccupations, but because they are the spheres where
her aesthetic sensibility found some patent and natural
models of representation that posed no resistance; they
were suitably fickle and at the same time recognizable,
universal. In this sense, Baroni has a firmly utilitarian
or charitable notion of her activity: to inspire, to teach,
to show, to circumscribe; it's a matter of words with
partially similar meanings. But as happens with many
artists, there is an uncontrollable zone of their art,
which is that of their own impact. And this impact
sometimes skews, maybe also disrupts, the apparent
or true simplicity of their actions.

That's why it seemed to me that the body of the poet Sánchez, lying in the coffin and dressed in his best safari jacket, shared some attributes with Baroni's figures. The work of laying out the dead and of adoring the saints probably led her to resolve her carvings that way, as if she were offering up wooden bodies to a versatile god of death, capable of welcoming almost any image. When I went out that dawn from Sánchez's wake, the avenue lined with giant trees seemed like a verdant tunnel that acted as an echo chamber for the litany of diminutive frogs, generally unseen but countless. Accustomed to nighttime vigils, Sánchez had been tortured for years by that earsplitting song; and now it turned out to be the music that the geography, let's say the native land, had chosen to bid him farewell. So when I left the wake and encountered the cool nighttime, in the middle of that down-sloping avenue that came from the mountains, I remembered that the saintly doctor, when he lived in Boconó, used to say that that city's surroundings were quite similar to those of Caracas. In a letter, he recounted that getting to a nearby town, Niquitao, took him three hours. As for me, when I did that stretch I made it in under fifteen minutes. Keeping this in mind his comment didn't surprise me; the territories kept their names, their best-known irregularities, perhaps the characteristics of their climate, etc., but they were essentially other ones, different within what was the same. The doctor underscored the mist, the low-hanging clouds and the icy temperature; he said the climate was so intensely cold that meat lasted three or four days without being salted. Anyway. He was amazed by the high plateau, by the pale color with which the only plant able to grow in those places, the famous frailejón, covered the mountains.

I mentioned farther back, almost at the beginning, a wooden figure in which the saintly doctor appears to be walking. He actually gives the impression of getting

ready to go up a hill, because his back leans slightly
forward. It's a normal-sized figure, of some thirty
centimeters, curiously wearing a turquoise suit. He has
his left hand forward and almost open, as if he were
about to ask for something, probably some coins, but
the arm is fast to his body, just like the right one. As a
result you think that in that also the mountain people are
reserved, in the allusion to alms and asking for charity.
His right hand, the one not asking, carries a doctor's
bag that's proportionally quite small, and which actually
seems to be a toy, or a school case in which to hold the
few medical instruments required for his now sparse
practice. In truth the bag is an attribute lacking in use
and persists as proof of the charitable and scientific
behavior of his period, shall we say, of physical existence;
and it has those dimensions, I presume, because it has
turned into a sort of amulet, or countersign, symbol of a
real situation that is nonetheless fictitious, like the small
toy purses, almost empty, carried by little girls in a hurry
to grow up.

This turquoise saintly doctor comes from Niquitao; as
soon as I saw him I imagined he was probably climbing
the steep pitch that rises from the highway alongside
the river. The doctor used these same words during his,
let's say, human life, 'steep pitch,' to refer to one of those
hillsides of thick greenery, probably that one where
the old man who made the piece lives today. Despite
his advanced age, Tomás Barazarte isn't resigned to
giving up his long walks when he needs to run errands
in Boconó. That was how I saw him the first time,
without knowing it was he: from a distance, a stubby,
wobbling presence walking on the side of the highway,
on the gravel shoulder a few steps from its verdant flank.
After meeting him and, over the course of a few days,
after having seen him walking more than once, when I
first saw the sky-blue saintly doctor that Barazarte was

kind enough to make for me, I noticed that he too, as Baroni with her Virgins and images in general, and as the painter Reverón customarily did with many of his figures, Barazarte had made this doctor in his image. The resemblance of their features is obvious, as also the bodily posture. Short steps, the head somewhat bowed toward the ground; the arms in particular turn out to be revealing in their likeness with the executor, so to speak, when they seem barely to swing and border on rigidity, beyond which walking would probably be a forced or artificial operation.

The last time I saw Barazarte was in Boconó, and the last memory consists precisely of observing him from behind walking, moving off toward the highway on his way home. He said goodbye in his brusque manner, verging on shyness; after that he simply turned around and began walking. The sky was overcast and, according to his impression, he probably stood a chance of rain along the way. He said nothing more before going off. Now every so often I approach the sky-blue saintly doctor and recall this affable but silent man. For some reason I'm not aware of, or perhaps without there being any reason at all, he has chosen to speak almost exclusively through his figures, which are otherwise not too forthcoming, either, but instead hermetic, of an austerity that makes them anonymous, even covert; this confers on them a more immediate presence or warmth, they're of an utter simplicity that doesn't preach and they belong to the broad universe of the undifferentiated.

At times, that kind of secondary plane Barazarte has opted for tempts me to think of a world of inverted orders, disconnected ones at any rate. The figures are less inanimate than what people suppose, and their creators, represented in an exemplary way by Baroni, Andrade or Barazarte, exchange life among themselves.

The pieces' passivity is deceptive; at night or in the
solitude of afternoons they move around and carry on
conversations, disagree and voice opinions, etc., one even
raises its voice; and they not only represent the person
their attire or physiognomy suggests, for instance the
saintly doctor, Bolívar or some Virgin in particular, but
display themselves, as if they were kindred individuals
with divergent whims, their own weaknesses, something
resembling biological families made up of similar
members with different characteristics. When it happens
and I think this way, in reality I discover no lesson and
barely arrive at any momentary conclusion. I imagine
the artists as accomplices of their work, restored to the
condition of hypothetical beings; not creations of their
own creatures, but materialized at one point of their
own imagination, when they must have conceived of
themselves as observers of what they were making or
would be making.

You go to Barazarte's house by going up an extremely
steep street. At a specific point you have to turn left. The
side street you encounter is even narrower and more
indefinite than the one before; a kind of herbaceous
conduit, the wilderness pouncing onto the pavement. I
realize that these details can prove a bit generic and for
that very reason irrelevant, but by mentioning them I
seek to pass along a recurring perplexity, that of having
been in a place that was both unique and indefinite.
From one point of view, it's the daily impact with which
the geography of this country confronts us, perhaps
because of the constant preeminence of nature, which
seems installed with excessive force, but above all
because of the tireless rhythm with which it unfolds.
The days almost don't change, the sun gets hot as usual,
the rains are continuous or absent, etc. Not to mention
the brightness and the raucousness. This has diverse
consequences, the most important by my criterion is that

the country is unrepresentable. I don't know about other people, in the past many have attempted it, but I've given up on it for some time. And I could not only be speaking of this country in particular, but also of some others. The more precise one wants to be, the more detailed and scrupulous with the nuances and contrasts; the more one hopes the flood of sensations will prove inspiring as a means of attaining an honest fidelity to the nature that displays itself in all its provocation; the more one wants to be mere instrument, seeking the propitious verbal deployment and the close reading of the event; the more there's all that, the result ends up being more incomplete and, above all, disintegrative. I therefore don't get my hopes up.

In a natural manner, people like Baroni know their own limits and a benign instinct almost always advises them not to go farther. She makes small statues that occupy two camps, those of art and of religion; at no moment do these works propose to translate a totality, nor do they even search for an argument in particular, or any affirmation, any meanings that aren't mystical or overly conventional. This straightforwardness seems to me revelatory. On the one hand, as I implied before, it shows the continuing validity of simple aesthetic styles, belonging to an old time, to a kind of initiation of the art, and on the other it projects, at least it's how I see it, a deep melancholy. This melancholy, it seems to me, is the viewer's contribution and relates to Baroni's sketching an argument about the world and no refutation; she and her work prove that representation is possible, that in this case the country offers to some its colors well-differentiated.

A few meters from me I have these wooden figures I've been mentioning from the outset, there are a number more besides, which I haven't remarked on and which

in general also represent the saintly doctor, diverse
Virgins or patron saints, rural characters, Simon Bolívar,
even President Hugo Chávez, of a protracted tenure, is
included with his baseball uniform from the Magallanes,
the team he's a fan of. All the figures are placed atop a
table where they almost don't fit; at times some fall off
the edges, because of the lack of space and the vibrations
of the floor. They make up an army of members who are
eloquent and mute at once, they convey solely their mere
presence, undaunted in the face of the company of all
the others. I begin to look them over and I get tired ...
Each one with its lone individuality, I think. And I get
surprised shortly afterward seeing not the image that
distinguishes them, which by now I know pretty much by
heart, but instead the silence they convey, unfathomable
but trivial, concrete despite being intangible. I look
on them as mute figures that display only their simple
presence. It's a kind of straightforward melancholy,
I don't know how to put it. The sadness of being
observable. The object put in place to be contemplated
at first produces nostalgia and secondly, owing to its
isolation amid the multiple gazes, conveys helplessness.

In his house Barazarte had a wooden gamecock flapping
its wings and bending its neck to the side. The movement
came out in the knot of the wood, whose twist Barazarte
had taken advantage of to produce an effect of tension, of
emergency or of alert, as if the animal had been surprised
or attacked without warning. This gamecock was a
discordant presence in that harmonious living room,
filled with plain, no doubt cherished furniture, at first
sight already jam packed with objects in their drawers
and on their shelves owing to the passing years and to
the abiding life at home, and also adorned, that living
room, with images of saints and family memorabilia.
There were other pieces by Barazarte, among them a
saintly doctor who was part of the household, more than

one and a half meters tall and also sky blue. Since the gamecock had a beak too long for its breed, I asked what animal one should suppose it to be. Everyone smiled, surely out of politeness, Barazarte first and afterward his wife, a few of their sons and daughters there with their families and, last of all, a nephew. The answer was that it was a gamecock, although long-beaked. Another thing about that animal that drew my attention was how it was painted. On practically the entire surface of its body it had a color similar to red and to brown, evidently a combination of the two with the predominance uneven, according to the part. Barazarte had avoided applying too much paint where its ribs stood out, he wanted them to reflect a corporeal tone. On its sides and on its prodigious plumage, considering that it was wood, there were also little specks in different colors, yellow, blue, white or red, minute freckles that perhaps sought to give the idea of vibration or luminosity, I thought. From the gamecock's head, actually from its crest, striations of slightly more defined colors went down its neck, which afterward, on the body proper and on the wings, mixed together and broke up, as I've said. That greater definition of the neck tended to enhance it, I suppose, to the detriment of the sections of diffusely colored areas.

It wasn't until quite a while later, when I witnessed a fight at a cockpit in the town of Paracotos, to the south of Caracas on the road to Maracay, a few dozen kilometers past Hoya de la Puerta, that I could clear up the enigma about the colors of Barazarte's gamecock and its exemplary verticality. I'm still not sure, but it occurred to me to think that that red-brown impasto, with more or less visible lines laid down on purpose, along with the small specks just mentioned, like freckles, were intended to reflect the movement of the gamecock in combat, the blurry-photo effect when these bodies are thrashing each other at great speed and are photographed. The

movement and the confusion, because the leaping of the
gamecocks seeking to thrust their feet forward and attack
makes them hesitate in a kind of volatile position, where
the lightness of their feathers, the clouds of raised dirt,
and the very wake of their movements, are combined.
You see them from above, a sort of toy coliseum where
the basic principles of perspective could be explicated.
Instinct leads them to be always alert and to strike
out at each other, after a mutual sizing up that can last
some moments, I suppose with no time to elaborate
any conscious strategy, a blind desire to kill and prevail
where technique is a natural virtue, if it exists at all.

Like so many places in the interior, there are two ways to
reach Paracotos: by the freeway or by the old highway.
From the cockpit, if you go to the remotest part of the
building, where a kind of roofed patio overlooks the
leafy background of the terrain, you can see, between the
trees and some abandoned concrete columns, a section
of the freeway, some two hundred meters away, with
the cars speeding past down there surely unaware that
they're being observed. The old highway, for its part,
has by now fallen almost entirely into disuse, and the
strip of asphalt has gone on disintegrating at the edges,
making way for wild nature; besides there's the overhead
growth of the plants and the bushes, which tend to
block the road. When the day's matches were over, or
at least after I had attended a good number of fights,
I took that old highway in the direction of Caracas,
and after going through various mountain passes and
meandering stretches, I reached Hoyo de la Puerta. In a
fairly brief span of time night had fallen and with it the
temperature had dropped; from the road you could see
in the distance the isolated lights of houses, a random
string of floodlights, etc., and surrounding each one
of these lights the black immensity made up of wild
hillsides or empty spaces. I stopped at an especially dark

clearing on the highway and began to study the sky, fairly empty of stars, at least of the ones we're used to seeing in the Southern Hemisphere. Just to mention something radically different, the inverted sequence of seasons never took me so habitually by surprise as the dissimilar landscape of the firmament; every time I looked up at the sky, as at this moment, I would feel a sudden fear: what I had expected to find wasn't there and I seemed to be inhabiting an unforeseen world until some moments went by, in reality it was something automatic, I'd take stock and then begin to contemplate with a touch of indifference that insipid, limited immensity, nonetheless as ineffable as the other.

While we were at the cockpit, during one of the intermissions I mentioned to my friend Barreto the story of the first miracle of the Virgin of the Mirror that Baroni had made, when by dawn she cures the mortally wounded gamecock. We were having some beers in the establishment's cantina; in Venezuela beer is the social conduit through which a good many conversations flow. He told me that while it wasn't impossible for a miracle to occur, experience showed that considerably more than one night would be needed to cure a wounded gamecock; but if it were mortally wounded only a miracle could save it. At times one wants to save a bird because one loves it, even though one knows it won't be any good for fighting and will remain sickly; but a gamecock incapable of fighting doesn't want to live. Along one wall you could see the row of cages, and to one side was the scale where the animals were weighed and the blackboard where the names were written and the matches agreed upon. Barreto also lives in Hoyo de la Puerta and he raises fighting cocks. Until a short while ago he watched the fights, but at a certain moment knowing them and seeing them die stopped being a tolerable possibility, and so now before one of his own cocks' fights begins he gets up and goes to the cantina to wait for it to be over. Another option he's discovered is to sell the birds before their first fight. At his house he has set up the cages on the ground, in fairly regular rows on narrow parallel terraces, because the land's downward slope is very pronounced. The name he's given to his house is halfway revealing: The Birdcage. At times a hen escapes and he has to go up some tree to collect it, or at times the chicks escape as well. The young cocks no longer escape because they are well secured in their cages.

Barreto's poetry books always have photographs in them. In one early book he's sitting in barbershop while they shave him. In another, from a few years ago, only his shadow appears, cast on the deck of a bridge over a river, next to the shadow of the photographer taking the picture. This book, called *Carama*, is an encomium to shadows and attempts to consider their one-sided existence, like ghosts abolished from the past. There he set out, let's say, to sing to his native village, San Fernando de Apure, surrounded by water and by savannas, a land where stones don't exist. Barreto publishes his books with a press that has him as its sole author, the *Sociedad de Amigos del Santo Sepulcro*, the Society of Friends of the Holy Sepulcher. All the members of this society of a Masonic origin are Barreto's relatives, now deceased; you can see the list of names on the book's flap. As its only living member, Barreto is the Society's spokesman. When this book came out, he took some copies to San Fernando to be sold there. He knew that many weren't necessary, besides it was a limited printing, of two hundred and fifty copies. But when he went back a number of months later, almost a year, he saw that not even one had been sold; among his friends and acquaintances from there he encountered an equivalent indifference. *Carama*'s thesis is simple and eloquent at once: the events of the past are surrounded by nature, those events now show up as nature, but as such they offer resistance; besides, nature itself, of which capricious and sporadic signals survive, belongs to the past. Poetry would be the discourse that delineates the forms of those hidden and contradictory shadows. It's a revelation with no desire for retrieval or encomium, and among sentiments accepts only melancholy and nostalgia.

I mention Barreto not just because of his admirable poetic qualities. On a certain occasion he took part in one of Baroni's performances. It concerned a wedding, which was going to take place in a Caracas museum where Barreto works and where Baroni's pieces were being exhibited. One day she set out to organize a wedding. She went into the streets to look for participants and got hold of a group of young people who would play the bridal party, afterward she got hold of the apparel, which would be campesino-style, those suits of ordinary cotton duck, etc. But when the wedding date arrived she still hadn't found anyone to play the bridegroom. And of course, Barreto graciously offered himself when he found out. Long afterward Barreto still spoke admiringly of Baroni's ease at becoming one with the action, as if it were a theatrical game; but at the same time he was observing her as the ceremony unfolded and saw in her expression a true commitment, as if something real were going on. Baroni was punctiliously decked out for that occasion, of course not in a conventional bridal gown. Later on she recited some of her compositions and the performance ended immediately after. Barreto then told me that the next day he asked Baroni the price of two pieces, saying he liked them and wanted to see if he could buy them. Baroni named him a high price, beyond Barreto's reach. So he asked for a discount. First he argued that it was a matter of two pieces; then, since that had little effect, he reasoned that she ought to give him a groom's price, since she couldn't charge him the same as everyone else.

To all appearances it was a good argument, because both carvings are now in Barreto's house, The Birdcage. One of them is a retablo where the religious scene issues from the natural surroundings, illustrated in this case with birds, trees and mountains.

When you speak with Barreto, the first response you're going to hear is always yes. For him a scenario of dissent is hardly imaginable; communication is related to agreement, and additionally to attention and deference. I've talked with him many times, and another thing that draws my attention is his particular form of discussion, which circles the reasons, states them, always leaves some possible definition hanging with ellipsis marks, as if being assertive were a lack of consideration for the other person. On occasion this must be particularly hard for him, because he possesses a varied and always thorough knowledge that expresses itself in almost incredible details. Perhaps that's why in his poems, which are descriptive and well-reasoned without being cerebral, you recapture the author's physical voice, even when it's looking to be ironic. In *Carama* he describes a curious game I wasn't acquainted with: 'a nimble-fingered man with a sharp knife / who played the fly: the players each / left a morsel of meat / on a table and sat still / the first one the insect landed on / that guy won.' It's a competition that belies the bravura inscribed on the sharp knife. Whether or not it's true that Barreto extracted these goings-on from old San Fernando newspapers, I always felt a kind of admiration for this game, which leaves to chance the animals' arbitration, as if it were an example of patience or Eastern wisdom. There are two other lines that are worth quoting, because they also represent Barreto: 'In their cages, the birds scratch with human / curiosity at every tiny detail.' It seems to me that here is one of his reasons for raising gamecocks, for Barreto an argument from observation.

So, in that wide opening I met up with on my way
back from Paracotos I had another of my moments
of mystical or natural exaltation. I was studying the
night sky, dark and transparent, a mixture of aromas
came from some orchards or nurseries nearby, several
dogs were heard off in the distance, etc. I wasn't very
far from the *cochinera* opposite Olga's house, where I
imagined the people from the area gathered together
and in some cases celebrating, etc. On nights like this,
I thought, the so-called world seems divided; there's
the whole more or less harmonious navigation of the
stars across the Universe, and there are the temporal
epicenters, I don't know what to call them, for example
that *cochinera*, the shrine of the saintly doctor or any
other place that operates as a nucleus of people. As
monumental as an epicenter may be, it is dwarfed
versus the other world, the galactic sky; yet obviously
not only owing to the difference in size but, as we
always think, because of the duration of the firmament,
which according to all assumptions will be distinct.
Nonetheless that duration is not a datum we can accept
as true, because the time span doesn't belong to the
sphere of our experience.

The Universe could explode the day after tomorrow
and ourselves with it, but in any case, if on the night
before I began to look at the sky in Hoyo de la Puerta
again, I would have the same sensation of smallness
and provisionality: the human epicenters on one side,
made to come to an end, and the stellar landscape on
the other, apparently wholly unharmed. And vice-versa
too, if someone could survive a stellar explosion, on
the following night he'd have a similar perception: the
everlasting above, and the provisional here below. For
that reason, I told myself, the difference originates in
the immensity's impact. What is immense seems more
permanent, as for example the seas or that sequence

of rolling hillsides, plunged at that moment in the completest jungle, but whose continuity over a hundred kilometers is intuited without problems. As you can tell, in that place in the middle of the night I had one of my habitual metaphysical collapses, I don't know if I should call them something else, and there I wanted to stay stopped forever, living as a half being, something like a vegetable or a motionless automaton, and to look without seeing all the time, immutable, obviously the same as those figures made by Baroni.

I've passed a good number of statues of the saintly doctor along the country's highways; at curves in the road, on natural or man-made promontories, on improvised pedestals, or on panoramic hills from which they keep vigil over or protect the well-being of travelers and people in general, or the silent landscape outright. And at this moment I dreamed of being one of them, it occurred to me to ask them to lend me the little life they had; a weak life, physically unverifiable in any case, but effective enough at least to remain endlessly in place, in a kind of constant contemplation, something similar to a spatial communion. It is relatively easy for an inanimate doll to acquire life and start moving, to loosen up its never-used joints, to begin to employ its thin whisper, etc.; I wanted the opposite, for a real person (and as far as I know, I was one) to assume a robotic doll existence and with that to see myself susceptible to a permanent and involuntary immobility. Always in the same place, facing the mountainsides and feeling the blowing of the cool, verdant breeze. It's true, at moments like this you allow yourself to be carried away by daydreams, and this dictated to me that I couldn't feel distant from the saintly doctor; not because a tie of devotion united me, or in any case not in the classical way, but because the life that sustained him attracted me.

The life provided by the gaze of others, a material made of nothing and nonetheless effective. I didn't think it was the best remedy for the despondency that had governed me for months, and which revealed itself in so many unforeseen ways, generally when I was unaccompanied and surrounded by nature and darkness, though basically through long mental soliloquies and abstract considerations that led me to nothing clear; but these reactions were the only thing I had on hand, they presented themselves as proof of a remnant of strength, probably the last. As they say, 'it's what there is.' It was what there was, I had nothing more on hand. In this way, I reached the conclusion that a good part of my liking for the saintly doctor was due to an outward appearance; the fact that he always looked pensive. Likewise Baroni's figures seemed to meditate in a particular way, and so I felt attracted to them from the outset too. Afterward what Baroni didn't make interested me, or what she made without noticing it, etc. A perfect fall into the abyss was what those figures had, because they reflected not concentration but absence, even distraction and a certain type of indifference; neither suffering nor tenderness; compassion would turn out to be, I think, an overly affected virtue. And at times I could even sense a certain obfuscation. The saintly doctor practiced a banal ascendancy, he was the idol who didn't bother to hide his feet of clay, and in this multifaceted way he was displayed throughout the whole land.

I stayed on the side of the highway for a good while then and afterward continued my journey. While one went on toward the city, the broad transverse valley of Caracas gradually appeared, sprawling and twinkling, with the luminous line of the peripheral road like a festoon at the foot of the mountain. The next morning I organized some photos that I'd had scattered around for some time. Some of them pertained to Baroni, and showed her in different situations. I've already referred to those where she's disguised herself as a rabbit and an iguana, also as a poinsettia. I found another one where she personifies the Virgin, dressed in white with modest embroidery and holding an actual child. She stands beside a bush and behind her you can see, by way of background, a typical Trujillan landscape. While Baroni looks at the camera, you have the impression that she's interested in something situated farther back, a bit above but surely distant. And just as in each of Baroni's photos, the preparation is apparent, the previous effort at home over the details of the clothing, in some cases over the makeup or the secondary elements or the assistants, in this case, for instance, the child who plays the role of the Child.

I separated out afterward other photos in which Baroni presides over a session at first sight public, with a train of people who get in line to talk to her. The place seems to be a museum or a cultural center, Baroni stands attending to them almost against the wall to one side. There is a common name for these images; on the envelope where I keep them I put, some time back, 'Baroni. ID Card Reading.' The person who for example in one photo is fifth in line, in another photo is being attended to; and so on for the rest of the people. People who arrive, move to the front – I imagine slowly – and afterward, once Baroni has already read their ID cards, are no longer there. This means that the photographic sequence belongs to a single day, surely a related event during some exhibit, because to one side of the photos you can see shapes that resemble Baroni's standard figures. At one moment it occurred to me to think whether the diagnosis hadn't been so negative as to lead each of them to do something mad after hearing it, so ominous was the effect of not finding in the photos the people I'd seen advancing step by step from the beginning. The ones for whom Baroni read their ID must be numerous and distributed over the whole territory, nevertheless I've only been able to locate one woman. On a certain occasion I asked her about the session and she refused to give me details, and she didn't want to tell me what Baroni had read to her or foreseen, either. She shook her head, a sign of hesitation, and immediately answered me with generalities: 'someday we'll see if it comes true' and similar things. That led me to think, in turn, that several of the people I asked had simply lied to me: they'd had their ID card read with Baroni but for some reason preferred to deny it. In any case it was an idea I had no opportunity to confirm.

In the sessions, Baroni holds the ID card in two hands and reads it with care, rather she examines it and focuses, I presume, on every detail. The photo, the line with the name, the number, the dates, nationality, expiration, in general everything: the printed national colors, the coat of arms, the watermark, the lamination. Each ID is a complex nerve system, or rather a unified weave, and as such sends out its own particular meaning which Baroni takes it upon herself to translate. It's not about reading the future, but analyzing the temperament of the, let's say, bearer of the ID card, weaknesses and strengths, the dangers they face and the reasons to be optimistic or cautious. Baroni has the palms of her hands open in front of her, as if they were a book, and in the center of the two holds the ID card. She has on the large pair of glasses she uses for reading or working, and in various photos you can see her talking, that is, reading the document of the person in front of her. They say she began reading ID cards a long time ago, even before she began carving. She already had the capacity to see inside people, also to heal. That developed upon her first return from death, and since then she has exercised it in a fairly constant manner, as long as her own health permitted it.

Although it may seem contradictory, the reading of ID cards goes back to the period of her blindness. Baroni was admitted to a mental hospital in Caracas, some 650 kilometers from Boconó, when she suffered a complete retinal detachment. I imagine it was probably a consequence of her nervous attacks, to call them by some name, especially the terrible head banging and jerking when her desperation became unbearable. Then she lost her sight and wanted to knit in order to earn a little money, because there was no one to help her. As I said above, she asked for needles and yarn and they gave her only yarn; that's how she began to knit by hand. Baroni's dexterity did not go unnoticed, and her state of deprivation came to the attention of the then First Lady, who in a charitable gesture decided to intervene by hiring a car to take her back to Boconó.

When she was back home, and despite having lost her sight, people came to her as much as or more than before. It's reasonable to imagine an increase in her fame, because blindness probably made her faculties more eminent. People would come and tell her their ID number, with which Baroni made the diagnosis: 'They kept telling me their numbers and I kept telling them things.' As you can see, the name was not enough; though it's probable that the information was rounded out with some contact through her hands. Sometime later she was denounced to the local bishop, but I haven't been able to ascertain the reasons; I suppose the ID card was a still more laical instrument of healing than medicine.

In Venezuela, the ID card is not merely proof of civil existence; it is also the document around which a particular type of subjectivity is created. Any transaction must begin with the presentation of the ID card; and on many occasions one must also leave, by way of proof, a copy of it. The locution 'photocopied ID' is very common, and a regular requirement in offices of all kinds, though there may be no certainty about the reasons for requesting it: whether to underscore the person's willingness, like a kind of confirmatory act, or simply to prove the document's existence. One begins to imagine the copies of ID cards there must be in the case-files and archives, in the drawers in houses and all types of offices; surely hundreds of millions. Given the frequency with which they're called for, it's reasonable for people to feel that their IDs and their copies were items inseparable from their own person, the same as a detachable DNA or a talisman against multiple fiascos. There is no commercial, civil, private or public proceeding that does not require a photocopied ID; existence and will are yoked there. Before beginning a transaction each individual looks in the mirror of his or her ID card, which operates as a safe-conduct in getting to the bottom of things. Another element that assists in the proliferation of originals and copies is their expiration, which is fairly frequent. You make various photocopies to have and so carry them around with you, besides that you keep a few as a precaution, because the copies turned out well, etc., but the moment comes when the ID expires, so that the photocopies are no longer any good. Then people are continually being left with the old documents and their copies, in some cases forever.

Two years afterward, Baroni recovered her sight thanks to the Virgin of the Mirror, as I explained before. And she went on making use of ID cards in her consultations, now reading them outright. To me it's admirable that she adopted such a civil resource, so to speak, and hence scarcely religious, and at the same time, owing to its use, so organic and intimate. I consider this to be another example of her enigmatic talent and of her surprising sensibility. When we were walking around the grounds of her house, moments before reaching the uncultivated part of the garden, I remembered these reading sessions, of which Barreto had on one occasion said to me that they always turned out to be infallible. But even though he'd been lucky enough to marry her, as far as I know Baroni never read his documentation.

I wanted to know what she saw in the ID cards; if she paid attention, as I supposed, to the variations in the object, not only to the photo. Some handiwork was involved in the manufacture of ID cards, so that the details of each one could be unique. In my case for example, on one occasion the clerk completed my ID card with another name. He should have copied the information from a form I had filled out. When he handed me the paper so that I could check it, still unlaminated, I noticed the error. He told me, in other words and making a little joke, that it was an important error. Then he took an eraser from his pocket and began to rub it out; he immediately put the paper back into the typewriter and typed the correct name using his index finger. The line ended up crooked, with the surname some millimeters higher than the first name, itself at an angle. I wondered then, accompanying Baroni through her garden, if that element could influence the reading that she would do of my ID card, and with that if my character or future would be revealed in another way. But I think something distracted me, surely the dog with his constant circling back, and this point ended up being another of the things that up to now I haven't asked her.

As I look at these photos of the readings it occurs to me to think of an agnostic seer, who has left behind some sort of paganism and establishes another, new one. People line up and proffer their document as if they were going to initiate a transaction. Baroni's mediation resembles that of the clerk behind the desk.

A short while ago I read a paragraph by the Uruguayan Levrero where he speaks of his ID card. He wrote in his diary: 'ID photos have a special something, I'm not sure what, impossible to find in other types of photos. They always reveal features or details that, for better or for worse, generally for worse, aren't revealed by other mechanisms.' It's characteristic of Levrero to slip in these comments that are assertive and hazy at once, with which it's difficult not to agree. Nonetheless he, too, discovered a subject matter that works without resting in the background of our civil identification, behind the photo, though we may abandon it. So much so, that this paragraph closes out his adventures in renewing his ID card: because he thought they'd keep his expired card at the government office, before going to exchange it he scanned it, seeking to preserve the mystery that was only there revealed. Among the photos we're accustomed to seeing, ID-style photos are of the oldest genre, or in any case of the most traditional genre, surely because they aim for a neutral expression of the face. They contain an indirect invocation of the past, together with the direct one, which is literal because it's chronological, and if they don't prove more revealing it's because of our lack of adaptability in examining them. Probably Levrero was referring to the aura; the aura of the past, the youthful aura of one's self in that photo from years past, etc. You can imagine him in front of the screen, in the silence of his home, during marathon sessions at the computer, at times feverish and at times tedious, absorbed before the old ID in the silence of his home. In that moment time is suspended, Levrero connects with the past, which rescues him and saves him, lends him the truth of that time reflected in the scanned image.

So I arrived that night in Caracas and I'm not exaggerating when I say I felt that something was coming to an end. A cycle was beginning to conclude, or rather an arbitrary stretch of the past and, along with this, its corresponding portion of reality was in retreat. Inhabiting the world suggests melancholy, I don't know if a lot, a little, deep or superficial, I don't even know if authentic or affected; and when we see that our place, the one we occupy, is imprecise and still more, undecided, without hesitating we bow to that melancholy. During the dry months fires used to break out on the great mountainsides. The smell of burning underbrush spread through the city, and in some areas you could see ash of an undefined color, containing minuscule pieces of carbonized matter. At that hour of the night the streets weren't more deserted than at an early hour: few people walking and an ever smaller number of cars. I inhaled the smell of smoke, and thought that the following day I'd find the remains of ashes all over. At one moment I raised my hand to my face and found something strange, a speck of charcoal. It may seem curious, but this verification in the sensory sequence, while incomplete, first smell, then touch, was so obvious to me that it erased any other thought that I had at that moment. It put me into a gap, a kind of waking dream of which I recall almost nothing.

Later on, in my building's narrow elevator, where only two people usually fit, I saw a brown paper bag, one of those in which bakeries customarily hand over bread or some prepared snack. The paper had been flattened against the floor, but before that someone had made it into a ball. My first thought was to associate it with the signals. I thought that a hungry or impatient neighbor hadn't waited to get home, and that the best way to expedite the snack had been to get rid of the bag. Or it could also have been a matter of carelessness. In any case that paper would be a signal, but depending on the case, of a different nature. So I picked it up from the floor with the idea of throwing it out later, but while the elevator was getting to the top floor I began to study it.

Obviously, I seemed to be peeping into other people's stories thanks to chance. But chance, I had realized long before, was organizing itself according to more and more predictable patterns. I mean, the whole of life was populated by details with ulterior meaning, so that the plainest activity or the most unreasonable digression bowed to the sequence of events and especially to their logic and foundations.

Let this lengthy preamble serve to make clear that I therefore felt no surprise at all when, getting off the elevator with the flattened paper in my hands, I recalled the painter Reverón's so-called masks and, a bit later, the example of Trujillo's capricious orography provided some time back by a friend, which I referred to earlier. So I decided not to be in a hurry to throw it out, I left the paper lying in the first place I found and allowed myself to extend the idea a little more: it occurred to me to exaggerate and to suppose that in the end the geography of the entire country could be represented as a wrinkled piece of paper, with its hollows, faults and irregularities. A piece of paper balled up and then immediately, but not completely, as I said a number of pages before, restored. While I was opening the window and the deafening uproar of the avenue came in like a gust of wind, I reached a foreseeable conclusion, but one that was of course difficult to prove: that with his self-portraits of paper, cardboard or fabric the painter Reverón had also made maps of the country. This, of course, in a metaphorical sense. I closed the window and went to the kitchen to get the paper to station it someplace, who knows until when. I succumbed, once again, to another recurring fact: my habit of keeping everything, because each thing is a kind of signal; an anchor, even an albatross, but also a promise owed by the past. At that moment in time the woman on the cross was looking out from her corner, next to the front door. And I had a brief thought dedicated to her before placing the injured ball in its precarious place: as I passed by her side I felt her squinting to follow me with her gaze. I should say it was another of the things that, at least until now, I've never been able to verify.